I0626020

LIFE
ON
THE
LAWN

by
KAY D
JOHNSON

Copyright © 2016 by Kay D. Johnson

All rights reserved. No part of this book may be reproduced or transmitted in any form or electronic or mechanical means, including photocopying, recording, or by any information storage and retrieval system, without the written permission of the publisher, except where permitted by law.
Names, places, characters, and incidents are the product of the author's imagination or are used fictionally. Any resemblances to actual events, locals or persons living or deceased is entirely coincidental.

Johnson, Kay D.
Life on the Lawn

ISBN 978-0-9952658-0-6 (pbk.)
ISBN 978-0-9952658-1-3 (ebook)

Chapter One

All knots and nerves, Emmett Sigmon, paced back and forth along the back fence line. His husky body wavered from side to side with each country-boy stride. His mind was fixed on his trade and the job he was about to carry out — today's auction. He only let his concentration break long enough to scrutinize the man that stood halfway down the same fence. Much to his relief, the man leaned quietly, studying his brown book and ignored him entirely allowing him to pace freely. But the fella's face was unfamiliar, and that made him even more curious each time he passed by the stranger. He inspected him closer. He noticed that the man held a rumpled up auction flyer in his thick fingers and was scribbling little notes in its margins — always a good sign to an auctioneer. In Emmett's head, he wanted the strange fella to stick around for the afternoon. By the looks of his physique and his secretive demeanor, he might be the one sure thing that would put some well-needed bidding thrills into this boring country-bumpkin auction and hopefully change it into something — well — downright feisty.

Reaching the end of the fence, he stopped his pacing and stared at the view before him. For well over an hour, people had been gathering in the backyard of the farmhouse. But to his big-business way of thinking, the number of people that turned out for the sale was looking downright sparse. He'd hoped for more. He decided it must be because of the weather conditions. Was it a good day or a bad day to hold an auction sale? Although it was bright and sunny, it was also hot, humid, and downright sticky. The kinda day when dogs didn't move, let alone bark, just trying to stay cool. It was a mere, ninety-nine degrees in the shade, with not even the tiniest touch of a breeze to relieve one's skin from the scorching heat. The air hung thick and tiring. However, a good day or a bad day, Emmett Sigmon didn't really care. Today's auction was scheduled for ten o'clock, and that's when it would start — ten o'clock sharp!

Many members of the crowd were dressed in as little clothing as possible, trying to stay cool while still remaining decently covered for the liking of their Southern modesty. A small sea of straw hats stood around the amassed belongings of Mr. Henry Phillips and his late wife, Virginia. Neighbors and friends stood fanning away the stifling heat with their pleated auction flyers. Some still scurried to examine the items one last time before the auction started. And a few last-minute bargain hunters registered with Miss Betty at the records table. The onlookers shared with each other the details of their daily lives and those of others.

Gossiping was one of the main reasons why many of them bothered to attend auctions in the first place. After all, where else, besides church, would you find that many people gathered in one spot, at one time, and at that time of day? And the biggest bit of gossip today was whispered from one curious ear to another. Who was that strange new man leaning against the fence? Men suspiciously frowned as they asked others if they'd ever seen him before, while the females, young and old alike, smiled and giggled about his eye-catching good looks. Mr. Sigmon glanced at his pocket watch to be sure that he wasn't late. In the nine years since he took over for his father, Mr. Emmett Sigmon Sr., he'd never been late, and he'd be damned if today would be the first.

From the shady side of the white clapboard farmhouse came the collective sounds of women quarreling.

Violet yelped, "Ouch! Lordy, watch the bumps. This wheelchair ain't got shocks on its wheels, ya know."

"Hey, don't be gripin' at me. It wasn't my idea to take this way. If you recall, it was me who said it would be easier and faster to take the regular path to the backyard. But oh no, you knew better, didn't you?" Frances's sturdy frame hunched over further to get better leverage behind the wheelchair and over the lumpy grass. At the age of sixty-two, it took her a lot more effort to do the simplest things than it used to. Behind her followed two more elderly ladies, both grinning and trying hard not to laugh out loud at the comical sight before them.

"Land sakes alive! It's as hot as Hades out here, and I merely thought that this side of the house would be cooler 'cause of the shade. Lordy, don't go getting your knickers in a knot." Violet slapped her legs to emphasize her counter-complaint. In retaliation, Frances purposely guided the wheels towards another large tuft of grass and shoved it hard over the bulge. "Ouch," wailed Violet as she jostled about in her seat. Pearl couldn't hold it in any longer, she let out a snort, and Ruby followed suit. The two of them stood half bent over laughing hard from the gut until they had to lean on each other and wipe tears from their eyes.

"What the hell is going on back there?" She struggled to turn the chair around by herself, but it wouldn't budge, "Turn this chair around. Right now!" Violet demanded.

With a gentle pat or two on her shoulder, Fran reassured Violet, "Everything's quite fine." She shot the other two friends a frigid look, hoping to shut them up. "They're just being ridiculously childish." She firmly held onto the handles of the chair in case she tried again. There was no way Fran was turning her chair around. If she did, Violet would realize that the tracks left by her wheels played connect-the-dots with the tufts of grass all along the house. Fran really wasn't being nasty. It was merely pay back for arguing against a plan that was completely and utterly logical. Although the path on the other side of the house was in full sun, it would have taken a quarter of the time and a lot less effort to get there. To Fran's way of thinking, if they had taken the path as she suggested, they would have been there by now.

"Sorry, I couldn't help it. The grass is so lumpy this time of summer." She gave Ruby a sideways wink, "Right Ruby?"

Ruby responded with a curl-bobbing nod, "Oh yes, this heat we've been havin' has dried out everything. Nothing but lumps and bumps in this lawn." She covered her mouth trying to stifle another round of giggling.

"That and Mr. Phillips hasn't mowed it in some time, bein' sick and all." Pearl gestured towards the lawn ahead of them with her long slender arm. She was tall for a black woman. Even though she stood inches above her friends, she never stooped down to their level. She was as proud of her height as she was of her heritage. When others asked how tall she was, she always replied, "Five foot, twelve inches." She enjoyed watching their facial expressions change when they figured it out in their heads.

Ruby stopped in her tracks, "Mr. Phillips wasn't sick. He just couldn't take care of himself any longer. He's at the Olive Grove Manor now. I know 'cause my daughter's his personal care worker. They pay her extra 'cause she's so good at her job." As she spoke, her strawberry blonde ringlets swayed and bounced. She was proud of her daughter's success and took every opportunity she could to darn well say so — especially when it came to her friends. At five foot, two inches, she was the shortest of the group of friends. But what she lacked in height, she surely made up for it in hot-tempered Southern attitude. Frances was next in height. She stood three inches taller with a meticulously braided salt and pepper ponytail that ended in the curvy hollow of her back. Everyone who encountered Fran instantly knew who she was and what she stood for. Frances Montague demanded respect, but never in words. Her blunt body language did the asking for her. If she disagreed with you, her steel blue eyes would promptly tell you so. And at that very moment, those eyes were telling Ruby to stop babbling.

Violet yelped, "Ouch! Watch it, will ya." She said it with a mixture of anger and apology. The apology was meant for Fran, but the anger was aimed at herself. She despised her wheelchair. It took away her freedom. She had to depend on others for help now, and she resented it. Violet's husband, William DuPont, passed away well over seventeen years ago, she'd been on her own and independent up until a mild stroke put her in a wheelchair three years ago. She loathed her life in that chair. Yet, she was lucky. She still had the use of both her arms and all of her faculties. God was cruel and kind, all in one final blow.

"Dang it, we're almost there. Just buck up for a few minutes more." Fran scowled at the others in attempts to shame them into assisting her with the chair.

Ruby was the first to jump in. "Oh here, let me help you." But she spoke as though it was her choice to do so, not Fran's. That was a satisfaction she was not going to let Fran enjoy. Ruby gripped the left arm, "Pearl, get over here and grab the other arm. We gotta get there by ten o'clock, or we'll miss something." She winked at Pearl to let her in on the joke. Pearl grinned back.

It was Pearl's turn to gripe, "The things I do for you bunch of weaklings." Without one spoken word from Pearl, she glanced at Fran who automatically moved to the side of the chair, switching positions with her. It was their usual formation. This was not the first time it took a group effort to get Violet where she needed to go. They didn't grumble though, after all, it could be any one of them in that chair. No one ever dared complain. Not even the day they carried Violet and her wheelchair up five flights of stairs to see a clairvoyant named Lady Carma. Frances thought the whole thing was a waste of hard-earned money and was nothing but pure foolishness. Yet, it was what Violet wanted to do, and friends stick with friends - no matter how ludicrous the adventure. The four ladies had been friends for more than forty-two years. Births, deaths, marriages, and divorces, they'd been there for each other. Even when they hated each other, they were still best of friends.

"One ... two ... three!" In a unison of grunts, they all shoved at once. The chair jerked forward and blasted across the grass. Violet bounced and shuddered wildly until they reached the corner of the house when Violet barked, "Stop!" Instantly the ladies dug in their heels, stopping the chair with a violent jolt.

"Why? What's the matter, Honey?" Ruby asked while straightening her aging, aching back.

"I don't want people to see ... this." She made a small swirl with her hand indicating the act of them pushing her. They all understood. No explanation was needed. Violet may have needed their help, but she wanted and deserved her dignity.

"'nough said," was Pearls straightforward answer, "Can you take it from here Honey?"

She held her head up high and pushed her chair forward by its wheels. "Damn right."

The ladies fell into another familiar formation. Ruby walking on the right, Fran on her left and Pearl behind the chair, in case she needed a little push to keep her going. The chair slowly made its way while she guided it around the tufts of brown grass.

In a low, soft voice she mumbled, "Thanks, girls."

At the first sight of the crowd, Ruby moaned, "Awe hell, they're gonna start without us." Mr. Sigmon was heading for the first item up for bid.

Violet pushed Ruby's rear end with her hand, "Go ahead. I'll meet you there."

"Well then 'thanks' right back at ya there Vi." She giggled, and with that, her and Fran high-tailed it toward the edge of the crowd. Curls and a braid bouncing wildly.

She looked up, "Pearl, you can go too. I'll be fine from here."

"Besides, ain't nothin' there worth rushin' for, I've seen it all before." She said it so Violet wouldn't feel awkward.

Mr. Sigmon announced the auction, "Lu, lu, ladies and gu, gu, gentleman, thank you for coming on such a hot day. Tu, tu, today's sale is that of Mr. and Mrs. Henry Phillips. All sales are final. All sales are to be paid in whole by six o'clock today ... no exceptions. And as always, absolutely no credit. Lu, lu, let's get started."

Emmett Sigmon was an oddity in the auctioning world; he was an auctioneer with a speech impediment. His stuttering started when he was four-years-old, after a scare with a rather randy bull that spring. His father feared that his only son would never be capable of taking over the family business as he had from his father. Then when he was nine, Emmett Sr. overheard his son mimicking him as an auctioneer to his dog in their backyard and without a hint of a stutter. From that day forward, his father trained him to carry on in his shoes. On his sixteenth birthday, Emmett Jr. called his first sale like a seasoned auctioneer. No stutters or confidence problems whatsoever. His words were strong and clear. The next day, his father took down the company sign and had it repainted to read, "Sigmon and Son Co. ~ Auctioneers."

"Wait a dang minute! I haven't got my number yet!" Fran yelled from the registration table, "It'll only take two shakes of a cow's tail. Hold on dang it." Betty filled in the forms on the tabletop.

'Bu, bu, but Mrs. Montague, it's ten o'clock ... sharp! And I'm starting nu, nu, now."

"Got it!" She hollered while proudly waving it in the air at full arm's length, "And it's my lucky number too." Her sign read #27, printed in bright blue numbers. "Okay Em, let'er fly, Honey."

"Why thank you, Miss Frances. I'm so delighted to have your permission to start my own sale." He shot her an annoyed look before beginning. "Fu, fu, first lot up for sale is this box of books. Who'll give me two-dollars?" His stutter vanished and so did the butterflies in his stomach.

In the back row, the man in the green shirt held up two fingers.

So the stranger did stay after all. That made Emmett smile a big wide smile. This could be a good day after all. "I got two. Do I hear two-fifty?"

The man in the red plaid shirt poked his card in the air, "Two-fifty."

"Okay, Bob's in. I got two-fifty. Do I hear three?"

The man in the green shirt jerked one single nod. A signal Emmett had become accustomed to seeing in his line of work. It also told Emmett that this stranger was a frequent auction bidder, another good sign for Emmett's business.

"I got three-dollars. Do I hear three-fifty?"

Bob, the man in red shirt, nodded a wild 'yes' again and grinned up at Emmett. He enjoyed it more when he could bid against somebody ... especially a stranger. It made it a challenge. More like a competition that needed to be battled out and won.

"Bob's got three-fifty. Do I hear four-dollars?" He waited, but no one budged, "Oh come on folks? Just four -dollars? Heck, the dictionary alone is worth six-dollars." He waited again and still, no one responded. He raised his gavel high in the air and gestured to everyone, "Okay then. That's four-dollars going once. Four-dollars going twice. Sold to #14 for three-dollars and fifty-cents." He banged the hammer on the podium. Emmett's gut sank. If the remainder of the sales were that minimal, he wouldn't earn enough profits from the entire day to have made it worth his time to come all the way there from the next county. He'd have to spice things up a bit and get them in the mood to bid — or at least bid higher.

"That's a shame. Three-dollars and fifty-cents for all those books? You'd thought they'd sell for more?"

"Not really. Remember Ruby, most of these folks can't read well."

"True 'nough." Pearl lightly nodded in agreement.

Fran pointed directly at the next-door neighbors, "But they can."

Ruby slapped her hand down, "Don't point, it's rude. Besides, this way we can talk about them without them knowing we are." She chuckled at herself for saying it out loud instead of keeping it in her head.

"Why? What's new?" Violet grinned up at her,

"They still feuding?" "Yep," Ruby's grin widened.

"What about this time?" Pearl bent down slightly so they could all keep their voices low.

Pleased with the amount of attention they were giving her, Ruby continued, "William wants to move back to the city."

"We should be so lucky," Fran muttered. William and Wendy lived next to the Phillips' farm and Fran lived on the other side of them. William Ottermen had been a thorn in her butt from the day he moved in. He didn't like her and the feeling was mutual from her. No one told her how to run her farmhouse — especially a man from the city.

"But they just bought a new tractor three weeks ago? Now he wants to leave?" Pearl couldn't believe her ears, "He's as silly as a school girl in a barn full of farm boys in springtime."

"Yep. Wendy told Daisy who told me first-hand that he's putting the farm up for sale next month."

"Hallelujah! There is a God and he does love me." It was a rare sight, Fran dancing a wee jig, "The day they're packed up and gone — the bourbon's on me."

"Lordy, you must really hate that man if you're willing to pay for the bourbon." In all the years Pearl had known Fran, she'd never seen her detest someone that much.

She pointed at him again. "Look at him, just look at him, standin' there like he's better than the rest of us. Just 'cause he's from the big city and we're nothing but dim-witted country folk. Ha! Danged ornery fool." Fran shook her finger directly at him, like a mother would scold her child.

"Sold to Bob ... again." Emmett looked down at him, "You gonna buy it all Bob?"

"Maybe? You gonna sell it all this cheap?" The crowd chuckled along with the quick bantering between the childhood chums.

"Nu, nu, next item up is lot #10." He held the next piece high so everyone could see. It was bone china white and rectangular in shape. The sides tapered down to a smaller footed base. The pattern was simple. Graceful yellow rose buds tinged pink with pale green leaves that sprayed behind the blooms. Oddly, on each end, a bulky triangular handle seemed out of place against the delicate rose pattern. "A complete set of china with matching stew bowl."

Violet couldn't believe her ears — a stew bowl? She had to correct him and his lack of proper information. She yelled up at him, "It's a terrine Emmett."

He turned in his hand, inspecting it closer, "Why, you're right Miss Violet." He held it up again, "With a matching terrine."

"And not just the usual one ladle. It has two matching ladles." Violet added with two waving fingers.

Emmett pursed his lips. Old ladies can be such a nuisance. "Mrs. DuPont, do you want to sell this one? I can go sit in the shade if you'd like." Again, the crowd of locals chuckled.

"Oh cheeky boy, you hush up now." She chided back with a half-blush.

With that settled, he cleared his throat and began again. "We'll start the sale of this terrine and its two ladles at one-hundred-dollars." He enjoyed it when the crowd chuckled along with him on the accentuated words. "Do I have the opening bid of one-hundred-dollars?"

Immediately, Bob popped his sign way up in the air, "One-hundred-dollars."

"I've got one-hundred-dollars. Do I hear one-ten? Who'll give me one-ten?"

The man in the green shirt signaled with his sign, but not amateur and animated as Bob had acted.

Life on the Lawn

Pearl nudged Fran's shoulder with her elbow, "That's the set I was telling you about."

After a 'down her nose' glance at the commonness of Pearl's nudge, she politely replied, "It wasn't me you spoke to."

"Oh, you're right. It was Joy I told, not you." With that, she stood quietly and listened with the others. She was actually waiting for one of them to ask the next obvious question.

"I've got one-ten. Do I hear one-twenty?" With a huge grin, Bob's shot his sign up again.

Fran testily prodded, "So are you gonna tell us or what?"

With a purely mischievous twinkle in her eye, she pointed at herself, "Me? Why that'd be gossipin' and you know I ain't a gossipin' woman. I don't like other women that gossi …"

Violet snapped at her, "Land sakes Pearl, shut up and tell us." The heat was getting to her, making her impatient and irritable.

"Oh yes," she smiled sweetly with triumph and nonchalantly pointed at the mound of china, "Well, that set of dishes was quite a prize for Ginia. You see, that snotty Mrs. Smitherson and Virginia got into a bidding war over them back in '82. They were part of Mr. Thompson's auction. Remember him? He's the one that died of consumption. Awful way to die, don't you think? With all those open sores and constant

14

coughing?" Fran blasted her yet another exasperated look, trying to hurry Pearl along. "They originally belonged to his great-grandmother. Come over on the

Mayflower or some such boat." "Ship," Fran corrected.

Pearl rolled her eyes at being put right by know-it-all Frances, "Fine! Ship." After a deep, calming breath, which she seemed to do a lot around Fran, she continued, "Ginia told me that the yellow rose pattern was quite rare and that only a hundred or so were originally manufactured. And that only a very few complete sets existed today." Ruby's head tilting posed the next question. "You see, they were trimmed in pure 24K gold. She said that most chinaware was destroyed during the civil war. Apparently, the soldiers scraped off the gold trim and melted it down into nuggets and traded them for money to buy food, whiskey, and whores."

Ruby growled out, "God damned war, ruined most of the beautiful things from back then."

"But the dishes weren't what they were both after. It was that terrine Emmett's holdin'." She pointed at it, "One day, Virginia and me were looking through her china cabinet for her autumn napkin rings, you know the silver ones with the oak leaves hammered right into the metal." Fran sighed at her wandering thoughts, urging her to get back on track. "She showed me the china set with that terrine and explained that there was only fifteen like it left in the whole entire world. And with those two ladles, she said it was nearly priceless."

"Really? That ugly thing?" Fran squeaked out.

"Ugly? Hush your mouth. That was Ginia favorite china pattern." Pearl grinned, "Hers and Mrs. Smitherson."

Fran set her jaw, "That is one woman I could never abide by. Mean hearted to the core." She shook her head in disgust, "Awful, awful woman."

"Well, both her and Virginia wanted it really bad. And they both knew the other wanted it as well. At first, when Emmett Sr. started the auction, the two of them matched bid for bid. Then the bidding got high and Virginia was about to give up, I remember seeing Henry come a runnin' from where the men were standing and whispered something into her ear. Right after that, she started bidding as if her pocketbook was on fire. Mrs. Smitherson couldn't believe it; she was being outbid by the wife of a farmer. It humiliated her. The wife of a factory tycoon losing out to a common farm woman. It seemed to make Mrs.

Smitherson wanted it even more. But Virginia bid her down every time. After awhile the crowd started to rebel against Mrs. Smitherson. Called her names like 'rich witch' and 'Mrs. Greedy.' They yelled at her to take her filthy factory money and go back to her almighty manor house. They were angry as all get out. Fists being shook at her and everything. It was something to see." She snorted, "She gave us quite the performance when she left too. Got all huffy and headed straight for their big black car. And as they drove away, you could see her throwin' things in the car like she was havin' a hissy fit. Ginia loved it. She said it made the winning of it even sweeter." She laughed harder and slapped her leg, "Come to think of it, we all enjoyed it."

"Would've liked to witness that myself," Fran pitched in.

"Me too!" chuckled Violet. "She was a spiteful woman. Always made others feel small and unimportant. Funny part was, she was the one who proved herself unimportant in the end."

Ruby tilted her head inquisitively, a red ringlet fell across her face and she blew it away with a sideways puff of air, "Wait? What do ya mean 'was'?"

Violet said delicately, "Was, as in she passed away."

"Hah! Now she's dead and she still can't have Virginia's china. Miserable old witch." Pearl sung in sweet soprano. "Ding dong the witch is dead."

"Shame on you." Fran scolded her, "She truly was a mean woman, but respect for the dead, please. No matter how much of a spoiled rotten, snake-in-the-grass bitch she really was." In true Fran fashion, she had managed to chastise Pearl, thoroughly lambast Mrs. Smitherson and all the while making herself appear saintly. She surely was the 'mistress of guilt.'

Ruby wanted to know all the details, "When'd she pass away?"

"Six days ago," Fran said it candidly.

Ruby protested, "Why didn't any of you call me? I'd went to the funeral with ya'll."

The other three glanced at each other. All three stood quiet for a moment. Violet finally said it, "None of us went. Um ... in fact, nobody went."

Ruby asked it sullenly, "Nobody?"

"Not a soul." Fran hung her head slightly in disgrace. "Only her immediate family and the office people from the plant."

Ruby's words were dismal, "But they'd have to go, wouldn't they?"

They all fell silent for a few moments. Each was thinking of their own mortality. What would their own funeral be like? Who would attend? And sadly — who wouldn't? After they exchanged reassuring smiles, confirming that they'd be there for each other, even in death, they turned their interests back to the auction.

"Two-hundred and sixty-dollars goes to Bob. Two-hundred and sixty-five-dollars? Do I hear two-sixty-five? I need two-sixty-five? Who'll give me two-sixty-five?" He shifted his interest to the man in green by the fence.

The stranger casually flicked his sign in response. Straightening up, he tried to scan the crowd for others that were interested, but the bright sunshine made it difficult to see. He shaded his eyes with his hand and squinted into the distance. He started at the far side of the crowd and followed the trail of hats. Halfway through the gathering, his eyes stopped at a group of ladies standing on the crest of the hill. He noted that they were roughly his age. He decided to keep an eye in that direction.

"Two-seventy. Two-seventy?" He pointed the gavel at Bob and up went his sign.

"Two-seventy-five?" He pointed at the man by the fence, who nodded once more.

"Two-eighty-five?" he spoke directly to Bob.

Again, his sign went up, but not as high as before, "Yep."

"Two-ninety?" he gestured to the other bidder.

The stranger nodded.

Emmett switched back to his friend, "Two-ninety-five Bob?"

Bob swallowed hard and softly confirmed, "Yep." He wasn't sure how high he was willing to take his bid, but so far, it was still within his budget.

Again, Emmett pointed the gavel at the stranger, "Three-hundred? I'm looking for three-hundred?"

"No," the stranger smiled, "T'ree-fifty." Up until now, he hadn't spoken a word. This was the first time that everyone heard the distinct accent in his voice.

At the exact same time, Bob whipped his head around and the crowd let out a collective 'Oooooh.' Heads in the crowd began to poke up over the heads of others in efforts to catch a glimpse of the stranger who was bidding like a crazy man.

Under his breath, Emmett mumbled, "Christ almighty." Emmett was thinking in his head that this could be a good thing, or it could be a bad thing. It was a good thing because he'd be earning extra money each time the stranger bid over the top. On the other hand, if the stranger kept bidding wildly, it might upset the locals and that could mean trouble later on. He'd seen it happen before, where the audience turned ugly and rebelled. And this particular crowd was known for its loyalty to its own community.

Bob's face drained white. Then it turned deep red as his blood pressure went up.

Emmett took a gulp from his water glass and cleared his throat, "Bob? Three-sixty?" He forced his hands hard into his front pockets, "Uh ... yep." He wasn't grinning anymore.

Emmett looked pass Bob's shoulder at the stranger, "I take it, three-seventy?"

The stranger nodded with a pleased smirk.

Next, he pointed at him with his chin, "Bob?" Bob wiped the sweat from his upper lip, "Yah. Fine. Three-seventy-five."

From behind Bob, the stranger cut in, "Four-hundred-dollars." He said it clear and poker-faced, without the excited passion bidding brought most folks.

Bob spun around in spot and he yelled through narrowed eyes, "That does it. Who in the hell are you, anyway?"

The stranger straightened up taller, "My name is Monsieur John-Paul Bordeaux." As a sociable gesture, he gave a small bow to Bob and the crowd, hoping to ease the tension.

Bob was further agitated by the fancy French name. Contempt crept into his voice, "Well Monsieur John-Paul Bordeaux, where the hell you from?" Emmett knew that tone of voice, trouble was definitely coming and that was the last thing he needed at an auction. He'd have to nip it in the bud. "Bobby, leave the man alone. He's got the right to bid on these items, just like everybody else."

"No, no, it is fine, Monsieur Emmett. I will answer de question. I am from Louisiana. I am 'ere on vacation. It is beautiful 'ere. So ... um ... quiet and friendly."

That did it. Anger jolted straight to his gut. To Bob, he was nothing but a snobby French outsider bidding on his things and he didn't like it one damned bit. "It was 'til you showed up." Bob's face turned sour with the resentment. He started to charge in the direction of the stranger when Sammy stopped him on the sixth stomp.

Sammy pushed his shiny silver flask in the path between Bob and John-Paul, making Bob stop short. "You don't want to do that; you'll get yourself all hot and sweaty fighting in this heat. Why don't you have some of my ... um ... water?" He added with a twinkling smile, "It's rather ... refreshing."

Nervously Emmett ordered, "Tu, tu, tu, take a swig of that water Bob. Cool yourself down. Either that or go home. My daddy wouldn't allow fist fighting at a sale and I won't either. You choose which you wanna do ... and make it quick."

John-Paul opened his mouth to say something, but Emmett gestured a stop with his hand. "Can we please get back to the bidding? Now, where were we? Oh yeah, fu, fu, four-hundred-dollars from John-Paul." He aimed his gavel directly at him, "Bob you in or out?"

Bob took another long sip from the flask and handed it back to Sammy, "Thanks."

"Anytime," Sammy fluttered his sparkling brown eyes at him, "and I mean, anytime."

Bob caught the brief flirty flash and for the first time wondered if the rumors about Sammy and Donald were true. Were the two actually homosexuals like everyone said they were? He took one step back from him and cautiously answered, "Um ... yah ... sure."

"Bob, you in or out?" Emmett saw the look Bob gave Sammy. He decided they'd have to talk about that whole situation later, from one buddy to another buddy. Because of his auction travels, Emmett knew information that others in this community didn't. He'd tell Bob what he knew about Sammy and make Bob swear on his mother's Bible that he wouldn't repeat it.

"Yah, I'm in. Four-ten."

Emmett once again looked beyond Bob to John-Paul, "And?"

He firmly nodded a polite, yes.

"Bob, fu, fu, four-thirty?"

He took out his dark blue polka dotted hanky and wiped his upper lip again, "Yah." His face was paler than before.

Emmett decided that this had turned into a nonauction and he had to re-establish the 'tongue of the sale,' "I got four-hundred and thirty-dollars. Four-forty? Do I hear four-forty? I needed four-forty." He pointed the gavel at the French man.

"Oui."

"Okay, four-thirty. Four-fifty. Do I hear four-fifty? I needed four-fifty. Do I hear four-fifty?" No stutter.

Bob muttered, "Holy Christ." He poked at the grass with the toe of his work boot, "Damn it all. Yah ... four-fifty." This time his face went red.

"Okay, four-fifty. Four-sixty. Do I hear four-sixty? I needed four- sixty. Do I hear four- sixty?"

John-Paul interrupted Emmett, "Monsieur 'awkins I will continue to bid until you 'ave bid no more. I 'ave no limit on my monies. I can bid forever. Please, let us not continue any longer."

Bob clenched his fists as he turned to face him, "The names Hawkins with an H in front of it. You could at least say it properly when you're talking ..." Then his face went motionless with a sudden realization, "Hey, how'd you know my last name was Hawkins?" He tilted his head and cocked an eye at him, "Mister, who the hell are you anyway? For real?"

"Who I am and where de 'ell I come from is not so important. Let us stop 'tis bidding. We should move on to de next one."

"He's right Bob. This could go on forever." He sent his friend a knock it off look, hoping to move on to the next item and avoid an altercation. "What do ya wanna do?"

The crowd was watching Bob closely. He felt the pressure of their eyes staring at him and folded under it, "Awe hell, let him have it." He wiped the beads of sweat from his forehead with his hanky, scrunched it tightly in his fist and stuffed it back into his pocket. And that's where his fist remained.

He couldn't quite read Bob's facial expression, so he thought he'd better check, "You're sure?" Emmett gave him one last chance. Mostly because he didn't want to hear about it every time he got together with him for a whiskey.

"Yah, I'm sure. Let Monsieur Frenchy over there have it." He added the last bit so that no one would think he was a quitter, "It's too damned big for my china shelf anyway."

"Okay then, sold for four-hundred and sixty-dollars to Monsieur John-Paul Bordeaux of Louisiana." Emmett slammed down the gavel and let out a sigh of relief. He had dodged a brawl and got a good price for it at the same time.

The crowd started to talk immediately. A mysterious Frenchman from Louisiana who outbid local boy Bob for a fancy china stew bowl; this type of thing never happened in a small town like Olive Grove. This was the stuff folk tales were made of. There were plenty of questions being asked and everyone wanted the answers. Who was this Frenchman, John-Paul? And why was he here in Olive Grove? How did he know about this particular auction? Why on earth did a stranger from Louisiana bid so high for an old stew bowl? What was so important about that stew bowl that he paid four-hundred and sixty-dollars for it? And come to think of it, why did Bob want a rose patterned fine china terrine? He was a bachelor that didn't even cook, let alone prepare a meal that would be elegant enough to be put in any kind of chinaware? And that odd detail made the citizens of Olive Grove chatter even more.

"Well, this is peculiar indeed," stated Violet. "Fran, what do you think about all this?" But Fran didn't answer her. "Fran?" She turned in her chair to witness Fran staring dreamy-eyed at Monsieur John-Paul Bordeaux. Violet couldn't resist it; she nudged Ruby with her elbow and pointed at Fran with her nose. In turn, Ruby nudged Pearl with her finger and smiled. They all smiled.

Pearl was the one to say it, "Why Frances Elizabeth Montague, what are you doing? Is that a man I see you looking at?"

Fran jerked out of her daydream, "What?" She refocused her attention back to her friends who by that time, were mischievously grinning at her. She blushed deep red. Being an overly proper Southern lady, Fran was mortified by even the thought of being discovered looking at a man in that manner. "I was just ... um ... looking at his ... um ... jacket."

Pearl grinned wider, "But he's not wearing a jacket, Fran. It's over ninety degrees out."

Fran's mouth fell open, "I was ... um ... just ... um"

At that exact second, all three of her friends burst out laughing. Fran decided that it, or she, was too damned funny to bother feeling awkward and joined them in laughing at the silliness of it all.

"Land sakes Fran, it's alright. It's been over four years. You don't need to mourn forever." Violet stroked her arm in a way that let her know that she understood what it's like to liberate the feelings of desire inside oneself after such a long time of being a widow. "Besides, that's one damned handsome-looking man, if I don't say so myself."

"Nice eyes," Ruby threw in. "They match his shirt."

"I wasn't exactly looking at his eyes," Fran tittered out. She pointed at John-Paul with her pinkie, "That ladies, is a sight that is as refreshing as a deep gulp of ice cold strawberry wine on a hot summer's night. Delicious."

"Amen to that." Pearl grinned too.

"Oh girls, she's got it back. Look at those eyes? They're simply glowin'" Violet smiled up at her, "And it's about damned time too." She poked her in the leg to emphasize the point.

"Amen to that," Pearl said for the second time.

Delighted by the possibilities, she forgot her proper uptight language and blurted it out in broken country slang. "Oh, girls, ya'll gotta find out where he's a stayin' at." Fran whirled around with her hands clutched begging-like and pleaded, "And by tonight."

With a tilted head, Ruby naively asked, "Why do you need to know where he's staying?"

"So she can accidentally run into him, of course," Violet chortled while teasingly fluttering her eyelashes at her.

"No, this time I think my car will suddenly get a flat tire right out front of where he's staying. It takes a long time to fix a tire." Fran's mouth formed a wicked smile, "Especially since my spare tire will unfortunately be flat as well."

"Oh, I can see it all now." Violet closed her eyes tight so she could describe it better, "That scrumptious man on his knees taking the nuts off with his long, thick tire wrench." Ruby let out a girlish giggle. "Why, you'll have to stand right beside him waiting patiently, won't you? Why that would make those lovely legs of yours right at his eye level, wouldn't they?" She lightly clapped her hands together, "Why, that boy is positively doomed. He doesn't have a chance in hell of getting away unscathed."

"Yep, those legs of yours have turned the heads of more men than that Amy-Marie Downey and she's twenty-two with legs up to here." Ruby drew her flatten hand up to her chin to emphasize their length. A look of pure envy washed over her face. At five foot, two inches, she wished she had Fran's long slender legs. She'd tease all the men she could with them. But she didn't and never would. For years, she had yearned for her body to burst into full speed and shoot up tall like the others. It never happened though. She was short and plump. And that made her heart sink a little. She shifted from one foot to another trying to hide the pain.

"It's all those stairs in her house." Violet grumbled, "She can't help but exercise them every day." She clasped her hands into one large fist and wedged them into her lap.

"Vi," was all that Pearl said. She snapped her mouth tight. Throughout their teenage years, there had been a long-time dispute and rivalry as to who had the best pair of legs, Frances, or Violet. Now it aggravated the hell out of Violet that she was the one trapped in the wheelchair with emaciated legs and Fran was able to keep her legs in lean, youthful man trapping shape.

"I'll go see what I can find out." Ruby pointed over her shoulder with her thumb to the tall woman wearing the bright pink polka dotted dress. "There's that horrible gossip, Penelope Baldwin. She knows everything about everybody. I'll go talk to her. That is, when she's done talking to Donald."

"She surely does know everything about everyone and that's what perturbs me most about her." Violet pondered with a scowl, "Do you ever wonder what she says about you to others after you're finished talking to her?"

"She ain't saying nothing about me, that's for damned sure. You see, when it comes to talking to that woman, I only talk about other people, that way she can't gather any information on me to gossip about." Fran was still eyeing the Frenchman. "So far, it's worked like a charm."

"Good thinking. I'll have to try it myself." Ruby folded her arms in annoyance that some people had that power and she could so easily be entangled by it. "But no matter how hard I try to not give it to her; she always seems to get some kinda information from me. That one is slicker than a catfish's whisker."

"I don't talk to her at all. Apparently, she doesn't like me. And yes ladies, I do thank the Good Lord for his mercy." Pearl clasped her hands in praise, "Blessed,
    I truly am."

But Violet knew better. Deep inside Pearl knew the reason why Penelope Baldwin didn't like her. It was because she was what Penelope called 'a Blacky.' And that brand of hatred cut Pearl to the core. Pearl took great pride in her heritage. Her ancestry could be traced back to North Africa where her family, by our standards, was nobility. It had pained Virginia to tell Pearl about Penelope's toxic label, but she did it because she loved her friend and Pearl had the right to know what was said about her. Virginia also fostered the fact that, witches like Penelope shouldn't be allowed to get away with such bigotry in these freethinking times. It happened when Violet, Pearl, and Virginia were in King's General Store. Evidently,

Virginia had overheard Penelope telling her other snooty friend that she didn't want to go to the other side of the store because that 'Blacky' Pearl was there and she didn't mix with her kind. And Virginia, knowing Pearl's temper, felt it best not to say anything until the little witch had left the store. At first, Pearl was infuriated and wanted to go after her, but Virginia held her in place until she calmed down. That's when she felt the shame. Not for herself, she was embarrassed of the human race that had to endure people like her and her kind. Later, when Penelope waved to them from across the street as though nothing had been said, they had to hold Pearl back from scratching her eyes out. Virginia held her back while Violet talked sense into her. They told her that Penelope Baldwin was nothing but a 'slave loving swine' and wasn't worthy of Pearl's time or emotions. To them and many others, Pearl Rutherford was a far better person than that 'hate filled white monster' as Virginia put it. They never told their other two friends and never spoke of it again. Yet, that painful scar remained embedded in Pearl's soul and burned for revenge whenever she saw Penelope Baldwin.

Fran commanded in a deep voice, "Well Ruby, get yourself going." She gave her a sharp shove on the back, "No time like the present."

Fran's bossy behavior perturbed her, "Holy cow! If you're in such a big fired hurry, go ask her yourself." Ruby didn't appreciate being ordered about by Fran and decided this would be an interesting time to stand her ground. She plunked her one fist on her hip, pursed her lips, and furrowed her brow, "And who died and made you queen? Hell, you didn't even say please."

They all watched as fury lit up Fran's eyes, "Oh, Christ almighty Ruby, you know what I mean. It's just the way I say it. I meant no harm." She crossed her arms in defiance.

Ruby stood facing her and heatedly shot back, "Ain't good enough. You're always treating me like I'm your personal lackey and I ain't." She jabbed her other hand on her other hip and intensified the conviction in her eyes. She pronounced each word separately and distinctly, "Now ... ask ... me ... nice."

Fran's face went blank in disbelief. In the forty-two plus years they had known each other, this was the first time Ruby Carson had stood up to Frances Montague. And she was doing it in public to boot!

"Ruby you're only teasing me. Right?"

She didn't ask her, she told her plain out straight, "Nope, ain't jokin' either. I mean it. Now ask proper like."

The other two ladies stood with their mouths gaping, waiting to see what would happen next. Could Ruby stand up for herself or would Fran subdue her the way she always did? Who would back down first?

"Come on Ruby, this is ridiculous. You know I meant no harm, it's just the way I say things."

She shook her head, "Don't care." She folded her arms firmly and leaned in towards her, "If you want me to ask that horrible woman where that scrumptious man is staying, you're gonna have to ask me properly and nicely. Damn it."

Fran looked at their other two friends with pleading eyes, "Girls, this is ridiculous." Before she could get any more words out, they both shook their heads back at her.

"Not in your life." Pearl waved her hands to halt her, "I'm not getting in the middle of this one."

Violet agreed. "Me neither. You're both on your own here."

"Well? I'm waiting." The fine lines on Ruby's forehead quickly became deep angry grooves. Now she was impatiently tapping her foot and drumming her fingers on her arm.

"I can't believe this? You're all turning on me. Well, isn't this just grand? After all the things I've done fo ..."

Ruby terminated her guilt trip with a single pointed finger, "Ain't gonna work." She wagged the finger back and forth at her, "Not this time." She demanded cold and forceful, "Now ask me proper."

The other two exchanged glances although no one budged. All four women were frozen in the hot midday sun — motionless, speechless. The Alamo itself hadn't suffered the amount of tension that surrounded them at that very moment. Fran stared at Ruby and Ruby stared straight back. Violet watched both of them and Pearl watched her. It was a silent stand-off that to each of them seemed to last for an eternity.

Finally, someone budged. Violet disgusted with it all, rolled her eyes in and grunted out, "Land sakes, Fran. Just ask her nicely?"

With mulish dignity, Fran tilted her head upward so she could look down her nose at Ruby. In a flat out defiant tone of voice, she simply dismissed her, "No. I don't think so. I'll ask her myself." Fran turned her back towards Ruby as she passed by her. At that moment, Frances Montague walked away from her friends, trying desperately to hold onto what little self-respect she could. The others paid no mind to her arrogance. They knew she'd be back soon enough and that they hadn't heard the end of this argument by a long shot.

"Stubborn old fool of a woman," Pearl muttered after Fran was out of earshot.

Violet slapped Ruby on the leg, "Good for you girl. You just did what I've been aching to do for about ... oh, say ... twenty damned years now." "Really?" Ruby said bewildered.

"Hell, yah! Me too!" Agreed Pearl and gave her a little shoulder hug.

"Yep," confirmed Violet.

Pearl warmly added, "You won, you know."

Ruby cocked her head, "Won what?"

"The fight." Pearl shook her head, "Girl, sometimes I swear you're retarded."

"No. Just a lady from the South." Ruby's eyes twinkled, "I know I won, but the question is, does she know I won?"

"Oh, she knows all right, but she'll never admit it. Danged old mule." Violet turned her chair towards Emmett, "Hey, he's at the lot I want to bid on."

"Lot #17, the Phillips' kerosene lu, lu, lamps. These are pu, pu, pure crystal, Swiss in origin, I believe." He held the one up high so that the sun would catch it at just the right angle. An explosion of miniature rainbows danced in the deep shadows of the large ash tree nearby. Emmett now knew he could raise the initial bidding price by the amount of 'awes' he got from the crowd. "The vu, vu, vase will be auctioned separately."

From the east side of the crowd came a man's trilling voice, "Come on Emmett, don't be a daft lad. They must go as a matching set. Virginia would've wanted them kept together. They were her mothers, you know, and she too would've wanted them kept together." It was strange to hear a Scottish accent spoken in Olive Grove. A Southern drawl was the normal dialect. Mr. Mc Fadden asked everyone at full volume while scanning his cane about them, "Do ya all agree wit' me?" The crowd noisily agreed with nodding heads and plenty of 'yeah' and 'oh yes, he's right' muttered loudly. "Aw, don't be daft lad, be selling them together then."

Emmett couldn't believe it. Now the crowd was dictating what items to sell with what lot. He shook his head at it all. At that exact moment, he came to the understanding that this was going to be a longer and more complicated day than he had previously thought. He took a deep breath and deliberately lowered his tone to an auctioneer's voice. With no more stuttering he started over again, "Alright then, that's two lamps and the flower vase. Opening price is seventy-five-dollars. Who'll start us off at seventy-five? Seventy-five? I'm looking for seventy-five-dollars. Who'll give me seventy-five?"

Everyone twisted about and stared straight at Bob.

"What ya'll gawking at?" He blushed deep scarlet before he held up his sign anyway. The multitude chuckled and turned their attention back to Emmett.

"Alrighty then. Bob's startin' us off at seventy-five-dollars." Under his breath, the front row heard him mumble, "No big surprise there." The few people up front laughed a little, but it died down quickly. He raised his voice so every person could hear, "Who'll give me eighty-dollars?"

"You who." Violet waved her arm up high, "Me. I'll bid eighty-dollars."

"Now hang on a dang minute. She ain't got a number," protested Bob.

"Is that right Mrs. DuPont? Do you have a number, ma'am?" He already knew the answer, but asked it anyway just to shut Bob up. Emmett was getting really annoyed with Bob's attitude and since he was controlling the auction, he thought he'd take advantage of his position and aggravate Bob along the way.

She put on her sweetest Southern belle smile, "No Emmett Honey, I don't. Would you be a sweetheart and get me one."

"Why, ma'am we most certainly can. Betty, you give Virgil a number for Mrs. DuPont." He peered over the top of the crowd to make sure Betty heard him. She nodded in agreement and Virgil stood waiting for the little sign to be delivered to Violet. "But let's start the bidding anyway." In the bottom of his sight line, he watched Bob's mouth clamp shut out of pure frustration. Seeing Bob flustered raised Emmett's spirits greatly.

Bob waved his dual fingered hand in the air and spluttered out, "But ... but ... but ..." Obviously, he wasn't thrilled that they were going to let her bid without a number. Bob stood there staring wide-eyed at his friend.

Responding to his protests, he mockingly cupped his hand behind his ear, "What's that Bob? Did you say something?" Emmett loved every minute of it.

"You can't do that. You just can't. It's unheard of. No one ever bids without a number. She should be turned down." Bob feverishly flailed his hands around in the air. "What's gotten into ya Emmett? You dun forget the rules or sumthin'?"

While Bob was busy acting like the village idiot, Virgil had already delivered Violet her number. As many times before, Virgil took his time talking to the lovely Violet DuPont. It was clear to everyone that he was smitten with her and she didn't exactly discourage his intentions either. Virgil had squatted down beside her wheelchair and smiled goofily up into Violet's rosy blushing face. Emmett had a fondness for blossoming romances and gave the old folks a little time to flirt. He shuffled some papers and drank some freshly poured water before breaking in, "Mrs. DuPont, you got your number yet, Ma'am?" Realizing that everyone was now looking at him and Violet, a rather jittery Virgil immediately straightened up and without saying goodbye to her, strutted back to the far side of the crowd. He folded his arms, indicating to Emmett that he didn't think what he did to Violet and him, was in any way humorous.

"Yes, I sure do Emmett." She switched her attention from Virgil and waggled a fingery wave at Bob. "Thanks for waiting, sonny. I really appreciate it, young man."

Bob's closed his eyes in utter disgust at the whole situation. "You're welcome Ma'am." Even as mad as he was, he remembered to respect his elders like his Mama had raised him to.

She smiled back. When the crowd had finally turned to face Emmett, Violet leaned into Ruby and whispered, "That Bobby child always was a little slow in the head. Takes after his papa, I reckon."

"Then we can continue? Let see, the last bid was ..."

"I bid eighty-dollars before we were so rudely interrupted by that young man over there." She pointed right at Bob. "But let's forgive him and carry on, shall we Emmett."

Emmett had to clear his throat to stop himself from laughing out loud. The old lady's gutsy sense of humor cut right to the comedic core.

Bob's mouth opened to say something, but realizing it would simply cause more teasing and at his own expense, he snapped it shut again. His face grew blood pressure red all over again.

"I'll try to." Emmett wiped the smile from his face with his bandanna, "Okay, I've got eighty-dollars. Do I hear eighty-five?"

Bob snarled out, "Eighty-five-dollars, damn it!" Two of women standing next to him stepped back a few paces.

"Got eighty-five. Do I hear ninety? I need ninety-dollars. Ninety? Who'll give me ninety?"

Violet gasped at Ruby, "Oh it's my turn, isn't it?" She poked her sign up in the air and hollered, "Ninety-dollars. If you please young Emmett?" The crowd mumbled their approval.

That was all he could tolerate. He switched into auction action immediately. "I got ninety-dollars. Who'll give me ninety-five? Ninety-five-dollars. Ninety-five, I need ninety-five-dollars. Do I hear ninety-five?" He looked at Monsieur Bordeaux, but John-Paul shook his head and closed his eyes as a signal of nonparticipation. Without a sound, Fran slid behind her friends.

Bob crossed his arms and sulked at him, "God damn it Emmett, ninety-five."

"I got ninety-five-dollars. Who'll give me one-hundred-dollars? One-hundred-dollars? One-hundred? I need one-hundred-dollars. Do I hear one-hundred?"

"Oh! Oh! One-hundred-dollars." Violet waved her sign frantically, "Over here."

For the first time, Bob watched her childlike excitement at bidding. It made him feel guilty. In all consciousness, he couldn't let her continue to bid with what little life savings she had. He winked at Emmett, "Oh, let her have it, Em." Then he gestured a goodwill smile in her direction. She returned it with a courteous nod.

"Two crystal kerosene lamps and one matching vase, sold to Mrs. Violet DuPont for one-hundred-dollars." Thankful it was finally finished, he hammered down the gavel so hard the handle vibrated out of his hand and tumbled to the ground. The crowd droned on again.

"Does that mean I got it? It's mine?" Ruby shook her head yes and Pearl applauded her friend's triumph. "I got it. I really got it?" Violet was so thrilled she jiggled about in her wheelchair almost falling out.

Ruby pulled her shoulder back, "Steady there girl."

"Bravo! Well done Vi." Fran stuck her hand out towards Violet for a congratulatory handshake, but Violet only stared up at her for a long hard moment. It was her way of standing up to her just as Ruby had. Frances Montague had gotten too big for her britches and needed to remember her place — that of being an equal, just like the rest of her friends.

Violet coldly turned her chair away from Fran and asked the others, "Now what do I do? I have no idea what I'm supposed to do now. I've never won before."

"When we're ready to go, we stop at the registrar's table and pay for everything we've bought today. So just relax and take it easy." Ruby patted her on the shoulder. "This is great fun, isn't it?"

Violet sadly said, "yah, but it's still a shame the children didn't want the Phillips family heirlooms." She was feeling a little guilty about winning, but in her heart, she knew Virginia would be pleased that the lamps and vase would at least stay with friends who cherish it as much as she and her mother had.

"Greedy little buggers." Pearl added harshly, "All they care about is getting their precious money. Greed is so ugly. Virginia is surely turning in her grave right about now."

Emmett announced loudly over the murmuring crowd, "Wu, wu, well that's folks, this concludes the fu, fu, first part of tu, tu, today's auction. Wu, wu, we'll now take a sh, sh, short break and return to the bidding in twenty minutes. Please make use of the coolin' shade and enjoy some that lu, lu, lemonade the Wrigley boys are selling. I know I'm gonna."

With those words, the overheated crowd made their way into the shadows of the nearby ancient

Chapter Two

The three ladies followed Violet's chair into the shade of the old apple tree that Virginia planted when Katie was born. It was covered with masses of undersized wine-red apples that weighed its boughs low down to the ground. Pearl had to hunch over so that her wiry hair wouldn't get caught in the tangled twigs of its long branches.

Since Pearl was standing behind Violet's chair, she had to lean her head completely back to look up into her face, "Hey, while you're up there, can you please pick me some of those apples. They make the sweetest apple pies. Remember the apple crumble Virginia brought to your sister's wake? She used these here apples. A quart should do it. If you can put them in my sack that would be terrific." She patted the bag attached to the side of her chair. Her face grew glum before she softly spoke, "I may miss her tasty baking, but dang it, I miss her even more. I'd give damned near anything to have her bake just one more of her apple pies and share it with us all. Just one more."

Pearl watched over her closely. If she let Violet get too downhearted, it was hard to get her spirits back up again, "No problem. Lord knows I'm right here and can't get much closer." She flicked away a skimpy limb that was sticking down lower than the rest, almost poking her in the cheek. "Us giraffes can do these things? A quart is that enough for two pies. 'Cause you know I'm coming over to play cards tomorrow and I'm gonna want a piece of that pie. I've had a craving for a piece of your double deep cinnamon bourbon apple pie." She plucked the ones with no wormholes, and that glowed vibrant red with ripeness. "Mmm … my mouth's watering already."

"Give me one of those?" Fran was trying to connect with them, but again, her words came out as a command rather than a friendly request.

Her words came out intentionally sharp, "Your arms broke? Get 'em yourself?" She refused to make eye contact with Fran, let her know she meant it. That was Pearl's restrained method of confrontation. No need for yelling, when silence served the purpose.

Both the tension and her own curiosity got the better of Violet. She whispered up to Fran, "Sooo … what'd you find out about the French feller? Where's he stayin' at?"

Fran frowned at Pearl and squatted down to answer Violet, "He's staying at the *Dragonfly Inn*. Been there for six days. Pays cash for everything — no credit. Eats at Southern Street Grill every evening around seven-thirty. And he never drinks alcohol with his meals, only after he's eaten and never more than two glasses of red wine. So, he's not a drunkard. Thank goodness!" she clasped her hands together in praise. "And according to Polly, who told Penelope, he is the politest man she's ever served. Good manners with excellent table etiquette. And apparently, he leaves hefty tips too. Shows he recognizes the value of a hard-working woman."

"That says a lot about a man. How he eats. You remember Tommy Rivers?" No one responded to Violet's question. "Sure, you all do." She flexed her arms in front of her to demonstrate his muscular physique, "He was good-looking, a jock and with tons of his daddy's money to throw around." Fran nodded her recollection of the young man. "Well after one dinner date, I immediately lost interest in him. Even though he was blonde, bronzed, and gorgeous, he was positively not the man for me." She negatively waved her hands over her chair, "Girls, he talked with his mouth full. Slurped on his coffee and then belched like he was at a hunt camp. He actually picked up his fork, held it like it was a shovel and proceeded to use it as such. As a lady of the South, I was so offended by his behavior that I felt the need to leave him sitting there alone. Lord knows I should have. And for the life of me, I don't know why I didn't. The final indignity happened when he plucked a shred of roast beef from the gap in his teeth, dangled it in the air with his fingertips and tossed it on his plate." Violet winced and shuddered.

"He didn't?" Fran sympathetically moaned, "Oh, how awful for you!"

"Oh yes, he did. And I was completely mortified." Dealing with the awkwardness of the confession, Violet cupped her hands in her lap as her face reddened, "I remember looking around the room, hoping that no one I knew was in the restaurant."

Pearl halted her apple picking to ask, "Was anyone there?"

"No. Thanks to the Good Lord, I was spared that humiliation." At this point, Violet decided she no longer wanted to be the center of attention and redirect it to someone else. Violet's voice turned into that of a teasing teenager, "But you like a man who enjoys his food. Don't ya Franny?"

For some reason unknown to the other two, Fran's defenses went up again. She felt anger well up inside her. "Why yes I do and what's wrong with that?" She knew damned well what Violet was referring to and she wasn't going to let her bring up that particular part of her past. Her eyebrows furrowed back at her, "And what's it to you now anyway?"

Ruby butted in before all hell broke loose again, "Holy Hanna. What's your problem now Fran?" Again, her motherly hands found their way to her curvy hips.

"Nothing!" She snapped, "Now just leave me alone, damn it!" With that, she abruptly spun around and stormed off towards the scattered auction items.

The three ladies looked at each other, but no one bothered to say a word about her little tantrum. Over the years, they had become accustomed to Fran's fickle temperaments.

As though nothing had happened, Pearl casually fastened the top of the chair's carrying pouch, "There. That should be enough for a decent pie or two. And I put in a few extras for eating."

Ruby laughed a little and asked her as sweetly as she could, "You ever eat one of those apples?"

"No." Pearl answered defensively.

"Go ahead. Try one." Violet's eyes dared her.

She couldn't let that challenge go by without defying it. Pearl pulled a deep red round one from the branch above her head and took a big bite. Instantly her face screwed up tight, her eyes closed, and a shudder jolted down through her body. A loud *Bluk*! was all she muttered before she spat the chewed mouthful to the ground. "Holy Hanna! That's God-awful sour!" The other two pointed and laughed at her. With one hand on her hip and wounded eyes, she yelped, "You knew it'd be sour, didn't you? Why'd you let me do that?"

"For the fun of it," sputtered out Violet, Ruby joined her with a snort or two.

"How can something so sour bake into something so sweet?" She spat out the last granules from her dry puckered mouth.

Ruby evaluated her friend in the distance. She pointed at her with her chin, "I guess they're kinda like Fran. Sweet when you add a little sugar; but sour if you neglect to. Sweetness needs to be coaxed out of some bitter things."

All three watched Fran pretending to examine Virginia's furniture, even though she had no logical reason to do so. She knew every inch and stick of that furniture by heart. After all, she had cleaned and dusted all of the pieces herself, off and on for over thirty years.

Ruby pointed with her nose, "What she up to now?"

"She's up to getting a date, that's what she's up to." Violet chuckled, "Lordy, she's still got it. Watch and learn girls. Franny the Flirt is about to make her first non-move."

Ruby tilted her head naively again, "Non-move? What on earth is that?"

"Just watch. I'll explain it as it happens." She leaned forward in her wheelchair, "Just look at her. Awe heck, in no time at all she'll be weedlin' her way into his head and then WHAM! ... that man's hooked. Faster than a large mouth bass on a fresh juicy worm. There she goes. Let the games begin," Violet hooted while rubbing her hands together.

Fran started by looking into a wooden crate marked Lot #29. It consisted of tin ovenware and a few casserole dishes. The pale-blue oval one evoked the delicious recollection of Virginia's chicken pot pie with cheesy tea biscuit crust. It made her mouth water as the memory rolled across her tongue. While bending over to examine its contents, she managed to arch her back. This move allowed her to push out her tush, making it eye-catching round without the deed appearing obvious to anyone else. In her youth, Frances Elizabeth Montague had come to realize that elegance would get you what you really wanted from a man, while shameful behavior only brought on chaos — troubles that were hard to live with and even harder to annihilate.

From there she moved further inward, nearer to John-Paul. She picked up and pretended to examine the oval gilded mirror that once hung in Virginia's front hall. For a split second, she spied at John-Paul in its reflection and immediately turned it away to admire herself in it. She straightened her clothing, especially around the cleavage of her white cotton peasant blouse. She checked her long braid by smoothing down any stray hairs and finger combing the large tassel of hair at its end. She peeked at him in the reflection once more. Still nothing. He was too busy looking in that darned little brown notebook of his. Somehow, she needed to catch his attention. In a flash, a sneaky little smirk slipped across her face. Slowly and precisely, she changed the angle of the mirror so that it reflected a shaft of sunlight to dance on John-Paul's bottle-green shirt. She watched his eyes take notice of the flickering light on his chest. He traced the sparkles of light back to the mirror and to her. His expression lit up, and he changed his stance from slouching on the fence to standing erect with squared shoulders. She immediately turned the mirror, and her attention, away from him. Quickly stuffing the mirror back into its crate, she continued with the game by ignoring him entirely.

"Stage one accomplished." Violet excitedly reported, "On to stage two."

"What's stage two?" Ruby asked curiously. Her curls bobbing about, as she knelt down on the grass beside her.

"Stage one is called the *baiting*. Stage two is *snaring*. Stage three is called ... there she goes! Watch her." She circled with her finger, "She's gonna work her way around him in a large ring, but without any contact and then *WHAM*, she'll move right in for a
slow, deliberate capture."
Pearl let out a low, "Humph!"

In high spirits, John-Paul took two steps forward but suddenly stopped short. He stood still for a few moments watching Fran. An enormous grin formed on his lips. He shook his head in disbelief and stuffed his fists into his jean pockets.

"Did you see that?" Pearl snapped a pointed finger at him, "I think he's done figured it out."
"By damned, you're right." Violet rubbed her hands together, "This is going to be an interesting day indeed."
Pearl blurted, "I've got five-bucks on John-Paul."
"I got Fran and let's make it an even ten, shall we?" Violet grinned up at her.
"You're on." Pearl was sure about placing her bet when she saw what John-Paul did next.

He walked directly to the opposite side of the auction area, picked up a wooden kitchen chair, plunked it down and sat on it with firmly crossed arms.

From that angle, the ladies could see his face and all of Fran's efforts in one panoramic view.

Sneaking a peek in his direction, Fran's manipulative amusement was replaced with a mixture of both shock and annoyance. John-Paul wasn't where she wanted him to be. How on earth was she going to encircle him when he was sitting on the outside of her circle? And worst of all, at that time he was watching her very closely. She wondered to herself, 'Did he know or did he not know what her strategy was?' Although she was curious, she knew better than to look fully in his direction. That action would only confirm what he might suspect what she was doing. While she mulled over in her head what to do next, she examined one of Virginia's cookbooks from the crate at her feet. In attempts to appear as though she was simply going to read its recipes, she leisurely opened its red cover. To her surprise, she discovered that she was the person who had originally given Virginia that very cookbook. Inside the front cover, Fran had once written a simple message to Virginia.

To a large kettle of life, first fill with desire,
then add one heaping cup of mischief,
along with five overly ripe friends.
Stir it up with trouble
to make one unforgettable half-baked adventure.
Friends forever, Franny.

"Well I'll be God damned," she mumbled to herself. Melancholy filled her heart. It hurt her to think that some stranger was going to bid on her book and the memories it held for Virginia and her. An overwhelming impulse rushed through her. She scanned the crowd around the trees and quickly shoved the cookbook under her loose cotton blouse. She scanned the crowd again to make sure no one had noticed. And that's when she saw Monsieur John-Paul Bordeaux grinning directly at her. "Damn it," she swore under her breath. It wasn't that he saw her take it that bothered her, her real problem was that he was sitting dab-smack in the middle of the pathway between her and the girls. Turning her back on him, she inhaled deeply and contemplated for a moment on what to do next. She came up with the only solution she could quickly think of — denial! Essentially, she would disregard him entirely and act as if she hadn't done anything wrong. Setting her Southern jaw, she made a beeline for her friends. She casually strutted pass Virginia's tall china cabinet; she slowed down at the table that held boxes of assorted glassware; gave Virginia's rocking chair one last push for old time sake; and as nonchalantly as she could muster, she strolled by John-Paul with her head held high.

He smiled up at her, "I saw what you did. You, Madame, are a thief."

She stopped dead in her tracks and wheeled around to face him, "I beg your pardon?" Her face held her best high-and-mighty expression. "Who are you to talk to me in this manner?"

Inside, he smiled to himself. In his head, he thought, *She fought back. I liked that in a woman.* He enjoyed a challenge, and it appeared that she did as well. "I am de man t'at saw you thieved t'at ... um ... um

... livre ... how do you say? Oh, yes ... book you 'ave under your blouse." He pointed directly at the spot where she was clutching it with her arms.

Realizing he was looking near her breasts, she colored deep pink while clasping close the front slit of her blouse. Pulling herself together, Fran refocused her attention back on him, "I have no idea what you are talking about." As planned, she promptly deigned it and turned to leave. But as with Fran's stubborn nature, she couldn't suppress her compulsion to correct his error, "And for your information, I am a Mademoiselle, not a Madame."

"Pardon moi – Mademoiselle for my um ... dumb mind," he corrected with a courteous bow of his head. "But Mademoiselle, if you do not talk with me, I will be forced to tell everyone t'at you are a thief. Please, Mademoiselle Frances let us not be angry against each ot'er."

Only one thought that raced through her head, 'How did he know my name?' She stared at him blankly, unable to find the words to say something — anything at all! This was not at all how it was supposed to turn out. It was John-Paul that was supposed to be awestruck by her, not her standing there flabbergasted and powerless to talk.

"Oh, what is wrong Mademoiselle? Has de Pussycat got at your tongue?" he raised one brow of his amused eyes, "No?"

She still couldn't speak. She was completely mesmerized by those brilliant green eyes. They seemed to invade her mind, to seep into her soul, paralyzing her body.

John-Paul stood up and offered her his chair by patting its seat, "Mademoiselle Frances, s'il vous plaît." His expression was pleading with her to cooperate.

Collecting herself again, she held her head up high, keeping her pride intact and plunked her bottom furiously down on the chair. She flared her nostrils in condemnation, "You ... you leave me no choice."

"Mademoiselle Frances I mean you no injury. I only want to talk with you."

"Fine." Fran crossed her arms in protest. "Then talk."

He smiled at her with his gleaming green eyes, "Why 'ave you thieved t'at book?"

Fran felt herself flush a heated pink, "It belonged to my friend Virginia. I gave it to her many years ago ... as a gift." She lightly hugged it through her blouse, "I thought I should keep it. You know. For the memories." Confessing made her uncomfortable. To hide the indignity of being caught, she squirmed in the chair and casually straightening out the wrinkles in her skirt.

From a distance, he could tell she was a fine-looking woman, but close up, he realized she was even more beautiful than he imagined. He couldn't help but notice how her bosom heaved with each of her tense breaths. Her skin looked silky soft to the touch. Her eyes, an intense blue-green like the sea, held both fire and fear. Although closed tight with annoyance, he wanted to kiss her warm rosy lips, over and over again.

He struggled not to show his true emotions he felt being so close to her. After a deep calming breath to collect his thoughts, he asked, "So you are sentimental? No?"

"Not usually. But this particular book meant a lot to her ... and well to me too. You see we had a huge fight, an argument really, and we finally made up because of a recipe in this book." With her fingers, she patted it through her blouse. A wide smile sweetly swept across his face. Realizing that she had already said too much, she abruptly cut herself off, "It's really a long story, and I don't wish to bore you with it."

Again, he smiled at her through glinting eyes, "It is no bother. I would ... um ... enjoy to listen about your life."

About her life? That scared her, sending a cold shiver down her spine. First, he knew her name and now he wanted to know about her life. Fear swarmed in her head. Fran loathed feeling afraid, to her, it meant being out of control, weak. Her automatic defense was to allow her fighting instincts to turn those meek emotions into protective anger. "It's also none of your damned business, Monsieur." She stated it bluntly to make her feels clear.

He knew he had gone too far and needed to retreat, "Mademoiselle, it is not necessary to be mad with moi. Again, I mean you no injury. I was ... um ... What is the word? Oh yes ... curious ... curious about what it is that you have thieved." He brushed a fly off his cheek.

Fran's defensiveness went into high-gear, "I haven't stolen anything. And if it's such a big damned deal, I shall put it back. Would that make you happy?" Like a cornered teenager, she bolted out of the chair and stomped back to the center of the auction area. Once again, she scanned the crowd for witnesses and seeing none, quickly yanked it from under her blouse and placed it back onto its box. She sent a sour sneer toward John-Paul as she walked past him to return to where her friends were standing.

With that unmistakable sign of his dismissal, he turned on his heels and headed for the opposite fence line. She heard his footsteps on the dry grass and spun around to find him walking away, leaving Fran staring after him. In her heart, she was sure she had made a disastrous mistake by letting her temper, once again, get the better of her.

"Um ... what just happened?" Ruby whispered to the other ladies.

"Damned if I know?" shrugged Pearl.

"Looks to me like the mighty Frances Elizabeth Montague has just been beaten at her own game." Violet joyfully clapped her hands together with approval. "And I'm lovin' it."

"Here she comes. Act normal," Ruby instructed under her breath without moving her lips.

"Us? Act normal. That'll be a stretch," teased Pearl.

The three ladies watched as Fran collected herself together. Cool and calm she made her way back to the group of friends and the shade of the apple tree.

No one said a word. Pearl picked another apple or two from a nearby branch. Ruby fussed with a ringlet in the mirror of her compact. It was Violet who scrutinized Fran closely, staring at her every move. Fran methodically worked her way around to the other side of the apple tree.

Life on the Lawn

"Whatcha doin' Frances?" Violet asked it loud enough for the girls to hear, but low enough so the rest of the crowd wouldn't.

"Nothing," Fran spouted out.

"Looks like something to me." Violet replied back.

She snapped at her, "What's your problem now? Can't a lady sit in the shade without being harassed?"

"Not if she's my friend and she's pouting, she can't." Ruby put her hands on her round hips again. "You want to tell us what's bothering you?"

"It's that fool Frenchman." She barked defensively, "I mean ... he's just downright irritating that's all."

Violet prodded, "Why? What did that *nice* Monsieur John-Paul do?" She put an emphasis on the word nice, knowing if she complimented him, it would get a rise out of Fran. Nothing made Fran talk more than when you annoyed her.

"Nothing." She folded her arms in a tight cantankerous knot. "Now leave me alone, damn it." Her face was fixed and furious.

Pearl glanced at Ruby and Ruby, in turn, looked at Violet. They knew very well that when Fran said 'leave me alone damn it,' it really meant 'please help me.' Clearly, they needed to make her talk about this situation — and about him!

Pearl nodded at the others, she would start the conversation rolling, "Yah, we saw you talking to him, and it didn't seem that friendly of a conversation."

"Stupid man." With that, she flung her legs out in front of her mimicking a sulking four-year-old.

With all the innocence she could muster, Ruby sweetly asked, "What was he talking to you about? I mean, him being a stranger and all. What on earth did he say to make you so mad?"

"Damned fool wanted to know what I had under my top, and it was none of his damned business. And it ain't any of yours either." She pulled her legs back in under her skirt and heatedly crossed them, Indian style.

Violet turned her wheelchair around to face her, "But what was under your top? I saw you take something out of that box and hide on yourself. What was it?"

"Holy Christ! Not you too?" In protest, she turned her shoulder away from Violet, "It was nothing. Now let it go."

Ruby quietly remarked, "That was an awfully big red nothing you shoved back in that box."

Fran whirled around and opened her mouth to say something nasty in reply when she realized there was no point in carrying on with the charade any longer. They knew something was up — they always knew when something was up. Now she'd have to tell them, and that was all there was to it. She inhaled deep and blew out some of her held anger before answering, "It was a book, okay?" Then she scowled back so that they wouldn't know they succeeded in making her admit anything.

Pearl added her own question, "What book?"

"Just a book. Damn it! What is this? An inquisition?" Fran put her back up again.

"Why, yes, it is. So, we can do this the easy way or the hard way. You feel like listening to us nag at you all day?" Ruby put her fist on one hip and frowned at her,

"We've got plenty of time, and you're stuck here until we leave in the station wagon." With her thumb, she pointed to Fran's farmhouse on the far off horizon. "That is, unless you feel like walking seventeen miles in this hellish heat." Ruby knew that would do it. She left Fran no choice; she'd have to reveal the secret item now. "So, spill it, Missy."

Fran's lower lip pouted out, "He accused me of stealing a cookbook. And I didn't do it." It was outlandish to watch a woman of her age behave so childishly.

"Um ... but you did, or at least you would have if he hadn't stopped you."

"Oh, horse patties! He didn't stop me. I just decided not to, shall we say, acquire it." There was no way Fran was going to let her friends think he won.

"Acquire?" Violet roared, "Frances you truly amaze me. You still believe there are two sets of rules in this world, one set for you and another for everyone else."

Pearl was determined to make Fran fess-up to what happened, "The bigger question is ... what did he say to make you run away from him like that?"

Fran's voice shrilled in defense, "I didn't run away from him."

Pearl shot her a 'be honest' look.

They all heard Ruby let out one of her guttural sighs of disappointment.

Violet pushed her wheelchair closer to Fran, "Land sakes, just tell us what happened. It's nearly time for the auction to start again and I'd like this all settled before then. So, spill it and now!" She was almost yelling, and people were turning around to see what all the commotion was.

Ruby shushed her, "Keep it down, dang it. You want everyone should hear?"

"Oh, all right." She got up from where she was sitting and beckoned them into a tight circle, "He said he would enjoy hearing about my life, and then he called me by my name."

Ruby naively asked, "So?"

"So? So? You don't get it. He called me Madame Frances." Her voice trembled and panic showed on her face. "Girls, how did he know my name?"

"Yikes." Ruby squealed, "That is mighty scary. No wonder you bolted. Having a total stranger call me by my name? That would scare the bee-Jesus out of me too."

Violet thrust her hand in the air to stop Ruby from nattering on, "Wait, wait, wait! Hold your horses. You said he called you Madame Frances, right?"

"Yes." She answered slowly and cautiously, wondering where on earth she was heading with her question.

"Well, if he knows so danged much about you, why'd he call you Madame when you're not even married?" Violet reassured her or at least made it seem that way.

Ruby proudly piped in, "And as you recall, Emmett used your first name when he asked you about your bidding number. Right?" Fran nodded yes. "Well, that's how he learned that part of your name." Her face displayed a huge confident smile. She had figured that clue out before the others had.

"True." Fran nodded again. She hated to admit it, but they were probably right, John-Paul had only gathered information about her and wasn't really to be feared after all. That fact was a relief. But she couldn't help feeling disappointed at the same time. Deep inside, she did want him to be interested in her — no — to be fascinated by her. But he wasn't. Her heart sank with the empty reality that the situation wasn't what she hoped it would be.

Seeing the ache in her eyes, Violet couldn't resist, she had to rub it in, "So your smiling suitor is not as enamored as you'd thought? Guess you let your imagination run away with you." Her tone of voice was not meant to tease Fran, but to demean her.

Pearl who had been silently studying the details in her head, finally spoke up, "That's not completely true. After all, he did make an effort to collect your name. And he did counteract your hunting game. So, in my opinion, I believe he really is interested in you?"

Before she could answer, Ruby squealed and gave a tiny bounce, sending her curls into a wild frenzy, "Oh my God, you do have an admirer."

Violet's face soured, "Oh please? It's not like he's asked her out on a date or any such thing. They've only talked. Heck, if you could even call that talking?" The color of Violet DuPont's jealousy for Frances Montague's love life was a cold, bitter green. Pretending as though what she had just said had no true consequence, Violet changed the subject, "Hey, Emmett's starting the sale again. Let's get over there and right quick." She swung her chair around and forced the wheels forward.

"I'm coming too," Ruby hollered after her, "See ya over there girls." She gave Fran one last excited smile before she fell in place behind the wheelchair.

Pearl and Fran silently stood in the shade, neither one said anything or looked at each other. They only listened to Emmett announce the second portion of the sale.

Pearl offered softly, "I know it hurts and I'm sorry."

Fran didn't answer. She only let her head slump down until her chin touched her chest. She tried hard to hold back her tears. Eventually, she pinched her leg to distract herself from her emotions.

Pearl gave her back a few motherly rubs and chuckled out loud at what she was witnessing, "Frances Elizabeth Montague don't give up so darned fast." She pointed with her nose, "Look."

Fran lifted her head to see John-Paul staring in her direction with a truly wounded expression. Her heart leaped at the sight of his misery. She got in two steps before Pearl seized her by the arm.

"Where in the hell do you think you're goin' in such a danged fired hurry?"

"To..." She started to explain, but Pearl broke in.

"Oh no, you don't Missy. You turn your backside right around here and look at me. Now!" she ordered.

For some unknown reason, Fran, a woman in her sixties, suddenly felt like a timid little girl and did exactly what she was told to do.

"I ain't gonna let you run yourself over there like some love sick teenage idiot. Now you listen to me good. You and Violet aren't the only ones that's played the man huntin' game. I've played it a few times myself, you know." She pulled Fran between her and John-Paul's line of view, shielding her own face from him. Pearl's face turned ruthless and harsh, "No woman that ever chased a man, caught him. You stand your ground and let him come to you. Remember, keep your power and never give it away. Especially to a creature that has no idea how to handle it." She gave Fran's shoulder a sharp shake, "You hearin' me Franny Girl?"

Fran was stunned. It had been years since Pearl had spoken to her in that manner. She swallowed hard at being scolded by her friend, "Yes. I hear you."

"Don't just say yes and not mean it. Now, take a minute to pull yourself together. Remember who you are Frances Elizabeth Montague. You are a polished Southern Bell and nothing less." She flashed her one of those smiles that only a true friend can smile after bawling that friend out.

"Yes Pearl, I do hear you." Fran closed her eyes, leaned her head back and took in a deep long breath. When she opened her eyes again, they confirmed she was prepared for whatever John-Paul would do next. "All set?" Fran didn't need to answer. Pearl knew by her grin that Fran was her poised, confident self again. "Good. Now let's get over there before those two idiots do something silly like buy a big china cabinet that we ain't able to haul home in the wagon." The statement made Fran spit out a laugh, mainly because it was the honest-to-goodness truth about their two sometimes dim-witted friends.

Chapter Three

Emmett was in high gear. "Do I hear fourteen? Give me fourteen. Fourteen. I got fourteen. Now I need fifteen. Do I hear fifteen? Fifteen? Fifteen? I got fifteen. Who'll give me sixteen? Sixteen? I've got sixteen. Now seventeen. Seventeen? I need seventeen." The bidding stopped. No one budged, no one motioned. "Seventeen? Last call for seventeen." He scanned the crowd for any signs of a bid. "No one? Okay. Final bid of sixteen-dollars goes to bidder #3." He slammed down the gavel with a sharp crack.

"Who's got #3?" Ruby asked on tiptoes.

"I think that's Sammy's number?" Pearl chimed in as her and Fran joined them. "He was looking at that chair plenty before the sale started. He told Donald that it would match their chaise longue. Something about the color being the same shade of salmon, but only paler and how it would complement the tapestries in the dining room."

"My, my. You do have good ears, don't you?" Fran snickered.

Pearl whispered, "I'm still trying to figure those two out. You know ... two guys living alone together. They've never dated any of the ladies from around these parts. And they decorated the Simpson's farmhouse in a gilded glory fit for the Queen. Don't get me wrong. It's beautiful. But too over-the-top for my taste."

Naively Ruby whispered back, "So?"

"So?" she widened her eyes at Ruby, "Holy Jesus! Just look at them. 'Gay or not too gay, that is the question.' I mean they're all giddy about a matching chair for their parlor." Pearl started to get overexcited, her arms flailed, and her voice went louder, "Kinda makes a body wonder."

"Hush up and keep your voices down. People are starting to gawk at us ... again," Violet scolded before she smothered a wide yawn with her hand.

Ruby squatted down beside her, "You getting tired Honey?"

"No. Just hot. Would you be a dear and put up my parasol? I think that would cut down on the heat. It's underneath my ..." Before she could finish, Ruby had it in her hand and was opening it up.

"There this should do it." She placed the handle in the holder on the back of the wheelchair. "Now you swing yourself to where the shade is best." Ruby was a natural mother, taking care of everyone, all the time.

"Thanks." She pushed the left wheel until the shade fell across her face and body. "That's better already." She stifled another yawn.

"She'll be out in no time," Fran whispered to Pearl.

"It's the heat. We get a breeze, but in that chair, she stays right out-and-out hot." She whispered back.

Violet eyes narrowed at them, "Yes, I'm hot and just 'cause I'm crippled doesn't mean I'm deaf!" She folded her arms and gave them that wicked look that only Violet could deliver. Eyes that seemed to pierce right into the other person's soul — sharp and deadly — like lethal little arrows.

"Sorry Honey, we were only worrying about you in this heat." Pearl softly smiled at her, hoping she wouldn't make a fuss about it.

"Emmett's got another batch to go." Ruby cut in, knowing it would stop the awkwardness. "Wonder what it is this time?"

Emmett cleared his dry throat and started the next round of bidding, "Lot #25. This lot consist of three crates of linen ... lace tablecloths, bed sheets, quilts, curtains, and the like. Bidding starts at twenty-dollars. Who'll start at twenty-dollars?"

Again, Sammy's paddle went straight up in the air, "Oh, oh, twenty," he squealed out. He was standing on his tiptoes, jumping up and down excitedly. Some of the nearby men took a few steps back. Other's exchanged disapproving looks.

"I've got twenty. Do I hear twenty-five? Who'll give me twenty-five?" Emmett scanned the crowd and spotted another paddle, "I got twenty-five. Do I hear thirty?" he looked back at Sammy, who nodded wildly and waggled his number. "I got thirty. Do I hear thirty-five?"

"Thirty-five." William gestured with his sign again.

"Okay, thirty-five. Do I hear forty? I need forty. Who'll give me forty?"

Sammy was whispering something into Donald's ear. Donald agreed by rubbing his hands together. Immediately Sammy turned about and yelled, "Forty please."

The cozy little display between the two men made Emmett's stomach squeamish, but 'a bid's a bid' he thought. That's what his father had taught him. It wasn't his place to judge others. And that money was money; it doesn't matter where it comes from. "Okay, I've got forty. Do I hear forty-five? Forty-five, who'll bid forty-five? I need forty-five."

Again, William's paddle went up, and his bid was accepted.

"Forty-five's good, on to fifty. Who'll give me fifty?" He looked Sammy's way, but Donald shook his head at Sammy, then he shook his head at Emmett.

Emmett had to confirm his reaction, "Are you sure?"

"Yep," Donald called back, "The quilt ain't worth that much. No one in the city will pay that kinda money for an old worn out quilt." Sammy lowered his eyes and blushed at the vulgarity of his partner's words. For all of Sammy's silly eccentricities, Donald was the opposite half, strong, unbending, and somewhat greedy.

Fran's back went up again, "The nerve of that little weasel of a man. Virginia made that quilt herself. She made it for Tommy when he moved into his double bed."

"Don't you mean ... Thomas?" Pearl corrected with a sarcastic tone.

"Thomas my big fat lily white Southern ass! That boy will always be 'Tadpole Tommy' to me. No matter how insufferable that child gets as an adult." As Fran spoke, her hands clenched into tight fists, "He was Tommy when I wiped away his tears and fed him bumble berry pie, and Tommy is what he will answer to, when he's talking to me." She shook her right fist in the air.

"Snot-nosed little twerp. The one time he was home, he called Virginia a 'farmwife' as though it was some kinda dirty word. Like it was something to be ashamed of. That rotten little bugger hurt Virginia's feelings and didn't even care. He almost felt pleased with himself for doing it too. Little bastard! He even called his Daddy a 'common farm worker.' Made me sick to listen to him put them down." With Pearl's head furiously bobbing back and forth befitting the temperament of the Black woman she was, she added, "But next time, I'm gonna let him have it." She stabbed the air with her finger, "No one, but no one, gets to treat people that way. Especially nice people like our Virginia and Henry." Calming herself down she lowered her voice, but muttered it to herself again, "Snot nosed little twerp."

Life on the Lawn

Ruby nudged her in the shoulder and pointed toward Violet. Pearl nudged Fran's arm and whispered, "Should we push her into the shade?"

"No. Leave her there. We'll only disturb her if we move her now," Fran whispered back.

They watched as Violet slowly fell asleep in her chair.

Pearl's heart went out to Violet, "Poor thing. She's so tired. She told me she hasn't been sleeping at nights. She said her legs ache in the heat, something about swelling with the heat and restricted blood flow. We should let her sleep for a spell."

"Don't worry. I'll poke her if she snores," Fran said with an amused, but sinister grin.

"Be nice," warned Ruby.

Pearl pointed with her nose, "Hey, that's the rug from the parlor."

"You mean carpet," Fran corrected.

Pearl rolled her eyes, "Same thing."

Fran touched her forearm, "Honestly Honey, you really need to expand your vocabulary. Give it some class and sophistication."

Pearl stuck out her tongue at her.

"Yah, just like that," joked Ruby. "Really mature and lady-like."

"Ya'll shut your traps." She folded her long dark arms in protest. She didn't like being teased and especially by both of them at once. "Anyhow, it's the carpet from the parlor. You know the one. It's got that stain in the corner."

"Yes of course … the stain," Fran confirmed with a firm nod.

Ruby tilted her head again, "What stain? I don't remember a stain."

"The. Stain." Pearl emphasized each word, hoping to jog her memory.

"What stain?" She was so annoyed that no one had told her about a stain, her words came out slow and heavily Southern. "I've never heard about a stain being on that carpet. In fact, I've never even seen a stain on it either. What are you talking about?"

Pearl jumped in before Fran could say anything nasty to her, "That's 'cause Virginia always covered it up. Sometimes she'd use a big piece of furniture or another rug to hide it."

"Virginia's sister couldn't get that stain out. Blood in wool is downright impossible to get out once it sets in." Fran used her know-it-all voice for the last bit.

"What blood? Human Blood?' Her curls whipped back and forth, "No wait, whose blood? And how come you've never told me about this before?" Ruby was clearly annoyed with her friends.

"Virginia's Uncle Paul's," Fran's body shivered slightly when she said it.

"Sick-O Bastard!" grumbled Pearl. She folded her arms over her breasts as though they still needed to be protected from his penetrating eyes. Even after their death, some men leave their filth and smut behind — lingering and tormenting the minds of their innocent victims.

"You can say that again," Fran nodded to her. She too felt the same need but refused to do it. To Fran that would be giving into it or him. Instead, she straightened her back taller and held her head a little higher in delayed defiance.

"Um ... I don't remember an Uncle Paul?" Ruby was confused as well as annoyed.

Pearl started off the story, "That's 'cause Cousin Grady, stabbed him dead in the parlor."

"Thus, the blood stains in the carpet." Fran thought that at this point, she'd better point out the obvious to the perplexed Ruby.

"Stabbed him? What for?" She had turned to face Pearl, and with the sun in her eyes, Ruby squinted up at her.

"'Cause of what he was doing to Great Auntie Molly-May."

Short little Ruby was on her tiptoes with frustration, "Oh for Christ sakes Pearl, just tell me it all. Stop giving me bits and pieces."

Unsure if she should tell Ruby, Pearl looked at Fran for approval. It was a family secret that had been hidden for years. No one talked about it. As though if they did, it would make it all too real again. They simply wanted to forget about it.

Fran's voice was somber, "Best you tell her. The cat's half-way out of the bag now anyway." She examined her feet, hiding her own feelings.

"Well, it was almost 20 years ago. Great Aunt Molly-May had come for a visit here at Henry and Virginia's. As it is well known, Aunt Molly-May had a habit of visiting each relative one by one, one after another. To this day, I'm not sure she ever really had a home of her own. She just seemed to visit people."

"Molly-May was sure a wild-child back then," Fran commented with an admiring grin. She envied Molly May's free spirit, a lifestyle Fran could never allow herself to experience. She didn't like being out of control — ever.

"She'd been staying here at Virginia's for less than a week, when a heat wave came through. Everyone else was out working the fields, so Molly-May stripped down to her slip and sat in the parlour listenin' to the radio. Her favourite song came on and she started dancin'. You remember the crazy way she used to dance, her hips all swingin' and swayin' like a hula girl. Some thought it was downright trashy the way she carried on. I thought it was wonderfully free, myself. Anyway, the next thing she knew she was grabbed from behind. It was Uncle Paul, and he'd been drinking. Remember what they always told us about Uncle Paul? 'Don't ever be alone with Uncle Paul ... especially when he's been into the hooch. He ain't to be trusted, Mama said."

"They say that when he was younger, he molested a couple of little girls over in his county. The police eventually ran him out of town. Too bad ... they should've shot him instead." Fran felt it justified in adding that last bit. She had no tolerance for vile men — or women — who hurt children in any manner, molestations, or beatings.

Pearl continued the story, "The way Molly-May told it, he had one arm over her shoulder grabbing her breast, and the other arm held her so tight she couldn't get away. She told the police she didn't know it was Uncle Paul until he spoke to her. She said she'd never forget what he said to her, 'I saw you dancing. I know it was just for me. You want my loving. Don't you girly' That's when she screamed and bit him in the arm. 'Cause of the pain, he let go his grip on her. She broke free and tried to run for the door. But he caught her by the arm and held on to her. Called her a 'teasing whore' and punched her full fisted in the face. She said once the stars cleared, she screamed again, 'cause by then he was shoving her down on the floor. He had her pinned underneath him and was trying to get his trousers off to rape her when she felt his body go limp and collapse on top of her. When she opened her eyes, she saw Cousin Grady standing over the two of them, holding a bloody kitchen knife in his hand. Molly-May said she started screaming again, making Cousin Grady dropped the knife. Cousin Grady told the police he rolled fat ass Paul off of her. He said he offered her his hand to help her up, but she slapped it out of the way. He said, she looked at Uncle Paul, and she went kinda crazy. She jumped to her feet, ran to her purse, pulled out that little pearl-handled Derringer of hers, ran back to Paul's body. She pointed the gun at his big ugly bald head. Grady grabbed it out of her hand before she could pull the trigger. If it hadn't been for Cousin Grady, she'd shot him dead."

"But you can't kill somebody twice," muttered Fran.

Ruby looked completely confused.

Pearl gave her the answer she needed, "Cousin Grady had already stabbed him to death. Once right through to the heart. Grady later told the police he was in the barn when he heard Molly-May screamin'. He got to the house just in time to see Paul pushing her down. Henry had forgotten a carving knife by the front door. Grady spotted it on the table and automatically picked it up. That's what Grady used to stab Paul in the back. Thank the Good Lord that Henry's memory was failing him that day. It might've turned out differently if he hadn't. In the end, the police didn't hold Cousin Grady accountable 'cause he was protectin' Molly-May from that no-good ugly pervert. Once the police investigation was completed, Molly-May decided to visit someone else for a spell."

Once again Fran inserted more of the details about Uncle Paul's criminal past, "We all found out after that he was wanted in two other states for brutally beating and raping five other women. Rotten bastard."

Ruby's face drained pale as she questioned, "So the stain on that carpet was from Uncle Paul's blood when Grady murdered him? Holy Christ Almighty, that gives me the heebie-jeebies."

Pearl confirmed it bluntly, "Yep, it's his."

Ruby said tenderly, "I always thought it was a beautiful carpet. The colors of the flowers were always so bright and fresh. Now I wish you hadn't told me. Now it's downright ugly."

Violet choked on a snore and stirred in her chair, "Damn it! I hate when I fall asleep in public like this."

She muffled another yawn, "What'd I miss anyway?" Ruby piped in, "The story of the infamous blood stained carpet."

She was still half-asleep and wasn't sure what she'd, in fact, had heard, "What in the Sam Hell are you talking about?"

Uncomfortable about the topic, Fran shuffled from one foot to the other, "We told her about when Uncle Paul attacked Great Aunt Molly-May."

"Oh, my ... that." Violet shook her head with compassion, "Shameful thing to happen to such a fine lady like Molly-May. She never was her same self after that. Squashed her spirit a might."

"Hush now, Emmett's wrapping it up," Pearl commanded. She thought it best to divert their attention to something more lighthearted.

"Okay, seventy-dollars. Seventy-five, do I hear seventy-five? I needed seventy-five. Do I hear seventy-five?" As before, he auctioned with no stutter.

Paddle #3 swayed high in the air.

"Okay, Sam's got seventy-five. Eighty, do I hear eighty? I needed eighty-dollars. Do I hear eighty? Who'll give me eighty?"

John-Paul nodded to Emmett, confirming his bid.

"I got eighty. Who'll give me eighty-five? Eighty-five's the bid. I need eighty-five-dollars." Emmett looked directly at Sammy this time, and as excepted, he waved his paddle with a wild flourish.

Next, he focused back on John-Paul, "Eighty-five it is. Do I hear ninety? Who'll give me ninety-dollars? Can I get ninety?"

In turn, John-Paul nodded back.

"Ninety-dollars. Do I hear ninety-five?" As previously, Sammy conferred with Donald about the price and as previously Sammy declined the bid with a sad shake of his head.

"All right folks, the bid is ninety-dollars. Last call for ninety-five-dollars. Do I hear ninety-five? No one? Okay then, sold to Monsieur John-Paul Bordeaux for ninety-dollars." The gavel slammed down on his podium.

"Good God he's gonna buy it all," chuckled Pearl.

Violet craned her neck, "Speakin' of buying it all, where'd that Bobby Hawkins get to?" She also managed a little smile in the direction of Virgil, making him turn red in the face.

Ruby tittered out, "He's busy chattin' up Suzanne Scott. And from what I can see, she ain't objecting to it either."

"Oh, that reminds me." Her face lit up, and she fiddled with her braid. "Guess what else I found out while I was speaking with Miss Penelope Baldwin? It appears that she's getting married in the spring." Fran had the widest smirk on her face. She was holding something back. She loved it when she knew something the others didn't. She'd make them ask her instead of telling them right off.

"What? To who?" Ruby's ringlet swayed as she asked, "I don't recall her dating anyone. Who's she marrying?" And if Ruby didn't know about it, no one did.

"She is betrothed to young Roger Rutherford." Fran mimicked Penelope's snobby mannerisms. She even managed to add Penelope's fluttery eye rolling into the telling, "You know, the son of Roger Rutherford Senior, owner and CEO of Rutherford Distilleries in Norfolk." Then she let out a roaring laugh. After a few seconds of thought, she was quickly joined by the others.

"Land sakes alive she's gone and done it. She's marryin' rich. I always knew she'd take the easy way out." Violet squinted up at Fran, "How old is this Roger-Distilleries-Junior anyway?"

"He just turned thirty-nine." Fran grinned like crazy. "She's only twenty-one."

"Holy wedding vows! She's done got herself a Sugar Daddy!" Violet shook her head in disappointment, "Pretty blondes always sell themselves short, don't they? It's a shame."

Pearl chortled out, "And to think, Miss Penelope Baldwin's marrying my darling Cousin Roger? Ain't that sweet?"

Once more, Ruby was baffled, "Cousin Roger? What are you talking about? No offense Pearl, but you're a black woman and well ... he's white. How on earth can you be cousins?"

Violet slapped the arm of her chair with total amusement, "'Cause their both Rutherford's, that's why." She turned to face Pearl, "And I believe that this is a noteworthy fact that should be pointed out to her royal majesty Penelope Baldwin." She slapped the arm again, "Only one thing though, may I please be there to witness it? It would make my day ... no, my entire year ... to watch that uppity little witch squirm."

"Um ... that would be immensely entertaining, but it would also be very embarrassing for Pearl, and you know it?" Fran stated it calmly.

"Why? And I still don't get it?" Ruby was utterly perplexed.

Even through her dark skin, Pearl's face reddened slightly, "'Cause Roger's Rutherford's Great, Great Grand Daddy was also my Great, Great Grand Daddy."

"How can that be? Like I said before, you're black and he's white." Ruby was truly a naïve soul when it came to understanding how the rest of the world conducted itself.

"'Cause his Great, Great, Grand Daddy owned my Great, Great Grand Mama." Her face turned a deeper red and her eyes filled with a human shame that came from her ancestors' harsh past. She blew out a deep breath before continuing, "And Master Rutherford took whatever he wanted, when he wanted. And that included his female slaves. He took pride in keeping his Negro women with child. Mama told me some girls were as young as twelve when he raped them. He didn't care. His way of thinking was 'when it came to slaves, it was cheaper to make them, than to buy them.' And with his white blood mixed in them, they weren't so damned lazy or slow in the head."

Violet shook her head in disgust, "Makes me ill to be a human being when I hear of things like that. Just downright sick."

In her own meek manner, Ruby remarked, "It seems to me, that's an even better reason to rub it in her face." She looked at Pearl with squinted eyes and spoke gently, "Especially after that horrible name she called you."

Pearl was mortified. Humiliation filled her soft-spoken words, "You know about that?" A knot formed in her stomach. How many other people knew about Penelope's name-calling?

"Yes. Virginia told me. She was some upset by it. Made me madder than hell too." Ruby's expression switched from heated to sly and cold, "Did you ever wonder why Penelope's bicycle tires kept going flat all that summer?" A sinister smile slid across her chubby face, "A little undetectable revenge can be rather satisfying. You should try it."

Pearl's mouth fell open at Ruby's admission of settling her score. Pearl closed her mouth and corrected her friend, "But that ain't my way Ruby." She shook her head, "If I did that, it would make me just as despicable as her. The good bible says to turn the other cheek and forgive those that need forgivin'."

A rather loud 'Amen' came from Fran's mouth. With that, several people turned around to look in their direction. Fast thinking Fran simply covered it up with, "Amen, what a beautiful day. Isn't it beautiful out today?" They nodded in agreement and returned to watching Emmett lifting up a rocking chair. She glanced at John-Paul's way, and he was still watching her. She gave him a delicate flirty wave. The kind Southern Bells are renowned for. He reacted with a wide smile. Fran's heart thumped wildly as she returned his smile. At that moment, there was no one else, but him and her in the world. No people, no auction, no friends — only him and her lost in their yearnings for each other. But Violet broke their spell.

Violet's screeched, "My Lord that's Virginia's rocker!"

"You mean Henry's?" Fran corrected.

"Henry's?" Pearl challenged back. "Why Henry's?"

"Yes, Henry's. It was passed down to Henry from his Grand Mother. Virginia told me all about it one day while she was nursing Katie in it. She told me that Henry's Great Grand Pappy made it for Harriet when she was carrying Henry. Old Jacob used wood from the family's hickory grove. He hand turned every spindle himself. 'A true labor of love' Virginia called it."

That made Violet furious again, "God damned little bastards." Violet slammed her fist into her numb leg, "Sellin' Virginia's rocker. They're nothing but heartless, greedy bastards. That's all those two brats are." Her face went red as her breathing became heavy.

"Vi, you calm down now. Your blood pressure is risin' again." Pearl rubbed her back. "Having another stroke ain't gonna make those two ingrates better people."

Fran interjected, "Um ... only one ingrate." She pulled away from John-Paul to face her friends, "I must make my opinion clear here. We all know that Thomas is a greedy, greedy man, but I believe Katie is another matter. From what Henry's been telling me, Katie's been pushed around by Thomas and her husband for quite a while now. In fact, she'd been so unhappy in New York that Henry had asked Katie to come back home and live with him on the farm. He told me she'd actually packed her bags and was heading for a waiting taxi when Richard stopped her. Apparently, he called Thomas immediately, and two of them went at her, bullying her into staying. According to Henry, Katie's too unstable and frail to stand up for herself and can't break free of those two male monsters. They control every move she makes. Henry believes that Richard and Thomas are in cahoots and have even made her sign over everything of hers to them. God damned lawyers aren't ever to be trusted! Especially if you're married to one."

"Poor Katie. I always thought that Richard was a little shady. Did Virginia know about this? Had she ever brought this up to any of you?"

"Just the once." Pearl counted with a single pointed finger, "But Henry told her to quit spreading gossip about his family, and she never mentioned it again."

"Well, she told me plenty." Violet's eyes narrowed with hatred, "Do you know what that lousy good-for-nothing son of theirs said to them? He said he didn't want to take over the farm and become a poor stupid farmer like his Daddy. He was going to be an accountant and make big money doing as little work as possible. No sweat and dirt for him. He was not getting his hands filthy with farm work." She threw her hands up in the air, "Then to boot all, Katie tells Virginia that she married Richard because she didn't want to end up like her mother, working her fingers to the bone and having to obey a man with nothing to show for it in the end. Well, she's sure found herself a real winner of a husband, didn't she? That Richard treats those fancy bred dogs of his, better than he treats his own wife. Almost serves her right, talking to her mother that way. Broke Virginia's heart, Katie did. To be disgraced by your own children." She shook her head, "Shameful, downright shameful."

"That can't be? I can't believe it. Katie loved her mother and this farm. What would make her act that way?" Ruby shook her head too.

"Richard, that's what happened. We all know Katie's been a fragile soul her whole life. Richard picked up on it right away and took advantage of it. Did you know Thomas and Richard tried to persuade Henry to sign over the farm to her, right when Virginia died?" All three narrowed in on her, "Yah. Here was Henry grieving over his wife's death and those vultures swooped in to feed on the remains of his life. How I hate that child." Fran clenched her fists, "If it hadn't been for a slip of the tongue, they would have got away with it too."

Ruby questioned, "What do you mean 'slip of the tongue'?"

"About two weeks after Virginia died, the three of them came for a visit. But they didn't stay at the farm. They stayed at the Dragonfly instead. Something about the smell and there being too many flies from the barn. It was Shirley who heard them scheming about how to fool 'old senile Henry' into signing the new documents that Richard had drawn up. It was a new will-and-testament signing over all rights to the house, the farm, and all of Henry's savings to his son Thomas." Fran repeatedly chopped the air with her finger to make her point, "If it hadn't been for Shirley's eavesdropping, they would have gotten away with it too."

"Little bastards!" Violet angrily punched her leg again.

"As soon as she heard what they were up to, she called Henry's lawyer, Tad Wilson and he put a stop to it. Those three must have been some surprised to see Henry, Tad Wilson and Sheriff Morton having tea in Henry's parlor that morning. Sheriff Morton guided Thomas into the back kitchen and informed him that they had exposed their plot to swindle Henry out of his assets and they had exactly one hour to leave town before he'd press charges on all three of them. He also strongly suggested that they not return to Henry's for a long while. Tad mentioned in a polite conversation with Richard that if anything was to change regarding Henry's will-and-testament, that there would be a full investigation as to why." Fran relaxed her body and laughed, "Shirley told me later on that when they return to the Inn, she had already packed their suitcases. She insisted they settle their bills immediately, while Douglas put their things directly into their car. She also joked she stayed outside waving goodbye, just to make sure they didn't steal anything before they pulled away."

"That's my Shirley!" roared Ruby. "She's one hell of a friend."

In the background, Emmett bellowed, "Sold." Emmett was getting hot and tired, so his gavel hit a little harder this time. "One rocking chair sold to Monsieur John-Paul for one-hundred and twenty-dollars." John-Paul nodded in agreement and switched his attention back to Fran once more. He sent her another tempting smile, and again, she smiled back. Virgil broke the stare when he passed between them carrying the rocking chair, adding it to John-Paul's already hefty collection.

"Looks like the games still going?" teased Ruby.

"No game. That one's too smart for games." Once again, Pearl pointed out the obvious to Ruby. "Now it's like being at Sunday school. It's the smiles and glances that count. Right, Fran?"

"Um ... What? Or I mean, pardon." Fran's face colored slightly, "Sorry, I wasn't listening."

"That's okay, I can understand why. He's worth losing yourself in." Pearl's face wore a little sinful smirk, "The man is truly an eye full of handsome."

She flippantly slapped Fran's leg, "Hell if I could get out of this damned chair, I'd give you a run for your money."

"You mean like the good old days?" Fran gave her a secret grin that can only be shared between lifelong girlfriends. "Didn't we give the boys a whirl?"

"That we surely did Franny girl. That reminds me, you remember Jude McCoy?" Violet moved her chair a little closer to the others.

"Jude McCoy? Jude McCoy?" Fran frowned, "Nope, can't say that I do."

"Sure you do. Blonde boy from the Todd Farm. Big blue eyes with big muscles to match." Violet outlined the shape of his square shoulders with her hands.

"Oh yah. Tall, tanned and tempting." Fran hummed approvingly.

Violet's eyes lit up, "Best rear end of that summer. All round and firm, a good handful."

"I agree with you there!" Fran laughed at her own words of admission.

"Well, I saw him in the city last month. He's old now."

Fran swept her hand over her face, "So are we if you hadn't noticed."

"No, I mean old. He's bawled with a pot belly on a scrawny body and wrinkled. He's old-man old." Melancholy filled her eyes. The lustrous memory of Jude McCoy had been tarnished - forever.

"That's a real shame. Lordy, he was an amazing kisser." Ruby let out a nostalgic sighed.

In unison, Fran and Violet yelped, "What?" "I said he was a damned good kisser. Nice soft lips. And he always smelled good too. Kinda ... manly like. It

turned my head every time."

The other ladies were completely stunned by her confession.

Violet quizzed her straight away, "Are you telling us you and Jude McCoy dated?"

"Dated? No, no, we just messed around a bit." She blushed through her own naughty smirk, "Anyhow, it was almost September, and I wasn't getting serious with somebody who was going to leave town in two weeks. Let's just say we both enjoyed the time we spend together." The others only stared at her. This was a side of Ruby she had never talked about. Feeling scrutinized, she promptly diverted the conversation away from herself, "Look Emmett's ready with another lot. Wonder what it is this time?"

Pearl, sympathetic to her awkward position, finally spoke up loud and clear, "Looks like a crate of books."

That caught Fran's attention. "Books?" She stretched high on her tiptoes to see inside the crate. There, on top, was Virginia's red cookbook. "Damn it!" She pulled out her bidding paddle and bolted to the front of the group, almost knocking over Peter Stone.

"Dang it lady, take it easy." Peter griped while regaining his balance.

She curtsied slightly, "I'm so sorry, Peter. I need to bid on this lot. My apologies, sir." Getting the niceties out of the way, she turned her focus fully on Emmett.

Emmett's voice bellowed over the noise of the crowd, "Lot #30. Lu, lu, looks like a box of old cookbooks and cooking magazines. We'll start the bidding off at fifteen-dollars. Do I hear fifteen-dollars?"

Fran's sign went straight up, "Fifteen." She yelled it loud so Emmett would hear her.

Pearl shook her head, "She's too eager. She should've waited and started at ten-dollars."

"I've got fifteen. Do I hear sixteen?" Emmett's voice was raspy with dehydration and over use.

A deep voice from the back sounded, "Sixteen."

Fran turned around to see John-Paul's paddle high in the air. Rage rushed through her. What was he doing? He knew damned well she wanted that cookbook of Virginia's. In the South, conflicts like this meant war. She cursed him under her breath, "Damned French bastard."

"Sixteen. I've got sixteen. Do I hear ..."

Before he could finish, Fran yelled, "Seventeen," catching Emmett completely off guard.

"Okay then. Seventeen-dollars. Do I hear eighteen? I need ..."

Once again, he was interrupted. This time it was John-Paul, "Twenty-dollars." His French accent caused the word 'dollar' sound exotic and foreign to everyone's Southern ears.

Emmett's heart leaped. This was turning into an honest-to-goodness bidding war — and over a bunch of beat up cookbooks. He licked his lips and clenched the gavel with his sweaty hand. "I've got twenty. Do I hear twenty-two?" He got greedy and raised the price by two-dollars instead of the standard one dollar, as they normally did for something so trivial.

"Twenty-five!" yelled Fran waving her paddle. The crowd gasped.

Emmett didn't bother to say a word. Determined to save his strained voice, he simply looked in John Paul direction.

"Thirty!" The crowd watched John-Paul. And then with a devilish grin, he sharply added, "Five!"

She stomped her foot and muttered, "Rotten bastard Frenchman." If he was trying to make her mad, it was working. But the stubborn side of Fran was determined not to lose her concentration and let him win. Gathering her thoughts together, she inhaled deeply and in her sweetest, most ladylike Southern accent, she calmly called out, "Fifty-dollars," as though the outrageously high price didn't matter at all.

The crowd let out another gasp that rapidly turned into intense whispering. Emmett couldn't believe his luck. The two of them were raising their own bids, and he didn't have to do a damned thing. He thought to himself, Things like this never happen in the big city.

"Sixty," John-Paul retaliated.

Fran was now beyond mad; she was infuriated. She let go of her Southern Bell charm and bid without hesitation or her customary lady-like formality, "Eighty-dollars."

"Ninety," he immediately shot back.

Saying each word loud and razor-sharp, she countered his bid, "One ... hundred ... dollars."

"Lordy! She's done lost her mind," hooted Violet, slapping the arm of her chair.

The crowd automatically turned their attention back to John-Paul.

He shook his head and sighed. He hated himself for what he was about to do, but it had to be done. He looked at Fran with apologetic eyes and slowly pronounced his next bid, "One-hundred and fifty-dollars." Inside he hoped this would put an end to the silliness.

In the crowd, the paper fans fluttered faster as they focused on Fran again.

At first, she stood absolutely still, frozen in place. Then her face drained pale and her body tensed. Fury filled her heart. She clenched her fists at her side and screamed, "You ... you ... bastard! You know I want it? Let me have it!"

Again, the crowd muttered and fixed their riveting eyes on John-Paul.

He only shook his head NO. Inside, he felt his heart sink heavy. If he could let her have it, he would. But that's not why he was here today; he had to win this bid.

As though the others didn't exist, she screamed at him across the crowd, "Bastard! You lousy French bastard!" Inside, hatred fused with her pain.

Ruby took a step forward to help Fran, but Pearl stopped her. All Pearl said was, "Wait. This is not our battle." And for once, naïve Ruby actually understood and stepped back beside Violet's chair. Violet's face reflected her own concerns for poor Fran.

John-Paul hung his head. Inside, he ached. He could see she was both angry and hurt by his actions, but he was powerless to change the situation. He had to win the bid on that lot — he had no choice.

At last, Emmett spoke, breaking the tension that hovered thick in the air, "The final bid is one-hundred and fifty-dollars." He loathed having to say it - knowing how much it would hurt her — in turn hurting him too. But this was his job. In his professional auctioneer voice, he asked the question, "Do I hear one-hundred and fifty-five?"

Everyone's attention switched to Frances Elizabeth Montague, and she felt the weight of their eyes on her. Humiliation mixed with the anger she held inside her. She couldn't endure it all — John-Paul's cruelty, the crowd glaring at her, and knowing she'd never own Virginia's cookbook. It overwhelmed her. With complete panic rushing through her, Fran turned on her heels and stormed off, holding back her tears. Ruby chased after her as she vanished around the corner of the house, leaving the crowd to speculate and whisper. They went from dead silent listening, to the deafening buzz of gossip. Their fans fluttered faster, and the small groups gathered closer together, keeping within earshot of each other.

Emmett had to finish the bidding. He pushed the air down with his hands, "Okay folks, calm down, calm down." He gave everyone a moment to settle. "As I said before, the final bid was one-hundred and fifty-dollars. Do I hear one-hundred and fifty-five? Last call for one-hundred and fifty-five." He scanned the crowd as he always did. As he knew would happen, no one responded. "One-hundred and fifty going once. One-hundred and fifty going twice." He banged the gavel hard, "Lot #30, sold, for one-hundred and fifty-dollars." He refused to look at John-Paul, mostly out of respect for Fran.

John-Paul stood motionless as he watched Virgil place the crate of books beside his other auction winnings. The book was still sitting on top, taunting his raw heart with it's fiery red color. He swallowed hard to hold back his own tears and pain. That was the part of his business he loathed. The pain of innocent people's lives being changed by limitless capital and the bidding power it brings. He ached for her.

Virgil walked back passed John-Paul, but he stopped short. Turning to face him, the old man narrowed his eyes up at him, "Why in the hell would you want to pay all that money for a box of old tattered cookbooks?" He crossed his arms and leaned on one leg, "And why didn't you let Miss Franny have them? They belonged to her best friend, Virginia. You should have let her have them." He set his face hard and shook his head at him, "And here I thought I liked you."

Emmett sternly yelled, "Virgil. Get yourself over here." With that, the old man narrowed his eyes at John-Paul and sent him a disapproving grunt before heading toward the podium and a waiting Emmett. As he stood beside it, he scanned the crowd looking for Violet and found her. Another set of smiles were exchanged, resulting in another round of redness.

But Monsieur John-Paul Bordeaux had greater concerns on his mind. What did he care whether an auction sale flunky liked him or not? It was thoughts of her, that filled his mind. His eyes burned from scrutinizing the exact spot where she had vanished behind the house. Secretly, he hoped that she would suddenly reappear and return to the auction. He studied the shadows a few moments longer, but she didn't re-emerge. His heart fell heavy while questions tumble through his mind. Where was Mademoiselle Frances? Was she all right? Would she come back to the sale? But most importantly, would she forgive him in the end?

Chapter Four

Ruby found Fran sitting on the ground, leaning against the side of the house. Streams of tears had left pink lines on her face. Ruby gently sat down beside her, without a word she reached up and put her arm around her shoulders. Fran crumbled into her lap and let it all go. Her body convulsed with the release of her intense pain. Ruby rubbed her back and let her cry it out. No words were spoken by Ruby, only compassionate touches to remind her that she wasn't alone and that someone indeed cared about her and was trying to understand her pain. Yet, in matters of the heart, no one could ever really understand someone else's pain.

Around the corner of the house, Pearl peered at her two friends huddled together on the grass. In the corner of her eye, Ruby caught a glimpse of her head. *Damn it!* she thought, *Not now, not yet!* Ruby knew the last thing that Fran needed right now was a lecture from Mother Pearl. What Fran needed was her calm delicate compassion to soothe her wounded heart— and pride. Pearl stepped forward, but with the simple 'halt' hand gesture, Ruby stopped her in mid-stride.

Pearl shrugged the question, *Why not?* Ruby only pushed the air back in her direction with a wave, hoping it would force her to retreat. But Pearl only shrugged again. Ruby, now beyond annoyed, shot her a *Not now!* look and signaled madly at her to go away. Pearl mouthed the word, *Okay, okay!* and left without making a noise. Fran was never the wiser; she had been too busy sobbing in Ruby's lap to notice.

Ruby fished out a couple of crumpled tissues and placed them in Fran's limp palm. Feeling the new sensation in her hand, the tissue distracted Fran long enough to pull her out of her crying jag. Her nose definitely required attention. Speaking through a wrinkled tissue, her words "thank you," came out muffled. She blew hard into it — twice. Then she handed it back to Ruby, but after realizing what she was doing, she let it fall to the ground instead. She let out a deep, shuddering sigh. Her voice came out timid and childlike, "Oh Ruby, what have I done? I'm so embarrassed. Why did I do that? I can't go back there. They will all laugh at me." She blew her nose hard again and started to stand, "I'm going home. Tell the others, so they don't worry."

"Like hell you are? Sit yourself down." She grabbed the back of Fran's blouse and pulled her back down onto her ass. She landed with a forceful thump. "You're not going anywhere."

Ruby's uncharacteristic behavior surprised Fran; this was twice in one day that Ruby had challenged her. And she didn't like it. "What are you doing? You can't treat me this way."

"Oh, yes I can. Twenty something years of friendship entitles me to do whatever it takes to get you through this ... this ... mishap." Her curls jiggled at the force of her words.

"Mishap? A mishap?" her eyes went wide with astonishment. She stabbed her finger into her chest, "That's an interesting word to describe me totally humiliating myself because of that man while being watched by everyone who knows me." A tear escaped out of the corner of her eye, and she ruthlessly wiped it away.

Ruby only laughed and mimicked her words, "Everyone who knows you? Hardly! Good God girl, stop being so damned dramatic. Why does everything have to be such a huge catastrophe when it comes to your life? It ain't as bad as you think."

Fran couldn't believe what she was saying to her. Now she was getting mad, "A huge catastrophe? Not as bad as I think? Have you lost your cotton-picking mind?"

She continued to chuckle, "No, but you have." She was doing all she could to keep the conversation humorous, knowing that if she didn't give into Fran's need for drama, she would get the results she wanted faster. And the fact that she was getting angry was a definite bonus. No one can cry and be mad at the same time.

Fran pointed her finger back at herself and screeched, "Me?"

"Yah. You!" She let out one last loud laugh, and then gathered herself together with a deep breath. It was time to get tough with her friend. She nastily crunched up her face and stared directly into her eyes, "Fran, what is it exactly that you think those people saw?"

She wiped her pointed finger toward the hidden crowd, her arm at full length, "They saw it all! That what they saw!" Tears filled her eyes once more. Again, the tissue sopped them up and away.

Ruby used her nose to point in the same direction, "Saw what? What did they see Fran?" She jammed a hand on her motherly hip, a sign of what was coming next.

"They saw me and John-Paul bidding against each other. That's what they saw. I can't go ..."

Ruby cut her off, "That's right. You just said it. And that's all they saw." She sweetly smiled at Fran, "Those people have no clue what's going on between you and him. All they saw was two people bidding on a box of cookbooks, plain and simple."

"But ... but ..."

"No buts. The only people who know the truth are John-Paul and us girls. And well, we haven't stopped being your friend because of the other stupid things you've done in your life, so why would we start now." She gently took hold of her shoulder and gave it a friendly little shake, "Stop and think about this and you'll see what I'm talking about." She rubbed Fran's back while she contemplated Ruby's words.

Fran tried to say it again, "But ..." and Ruby only shook her head *No* and got to her feet.

"Come on. We've got an auction to finish." She held out her hand to help her up, "Coming?"

Still not sure of Ruby's theory, "But they ... and he ..."

She offered her the same insistent open hand again, "Coming?" Ruby sent her a reassuring smile that she was right and that everything was going to be okay, "Come on, we'll get some lemonade. It's hot as Hades today, and my mouth's as dry as the dust on an old wagon wheel."

Fran cautiously took her hand; letting Ruby yank her upright. Her eyes showed the dread she held inside. Fran took great pride in conducting herself in a proper manner at all times. And it was quite clear she hadn't behaved that way today. What would the people do and say? How was she ever going to live this down? Ruby just stood there with that same reassuring expression. She let out another held breath, "You're sure no one will laugh?"

"Who cares if they do? I mean, are you remembering who's in that crowd? Lordy, they're all country pumpkins and holler hicks. They're well beneath us fine, dignified ladies. So, who cares what they think? Oh, just minute, you've got grass on your bottom," she carefully brushed it away without smearing it into the fabric. "Deep breath now." Ruby raised her head high and called over her shoulder as she walked towards the sale, "Come on. Let's go."

Fran straightened her clothing, checking for more strands of grass, then chased behind her like a toddler, "Wait up, dang it."

As they reached the corner, Ruby stopped long enough to give her arm a squeeze, "Deep breath now. You can do this."

Fran inhaled deeply and put on a cheery smile, "I'm good now. Thanks, Honey. You're such a good friend to me."

"You're welcome." Ruby's eyes shifted to mischievous, "Oh yah, and by the way ... last one there is a rotten egg."

"What?" The words didn't make sense coming from a full-grown chubby woman.

Within a second, Ruby started running towards the crowd. "I'm gonna win! I'm gonna win!" she teased behind her. It was hard to tell which jiggled more, her hips or her curls, but either way, she was running like a mad man.

Fran mumbled to herself, "She's plum lost her mind." But her persistent need to be the winner overtook her, and she chased after her with the same childish sprint. "Not if I can help it?" she hollered back. It felt light-hearted and carefree to run after her. In her mind, she let go of the pain and the worry and pretended she was Aunt Molly-May — carefree and spontaneous.

Ruby got there first, slamming into Pearl, almost knocking her over.

Pearl caught her balance, "Hey, watch it?"

"I win! I win!" Ruby pointed at Fran, "You're the rotten egg!"

Fran was huffing and puffing by the time she reached the girls, "You ... left ... before me ... and ... so ... it doesn't ... count." She gasped deeply for air in between words.

Violet laughed, "You still can't lose gracefully, can ya Franny?"

"Nope, because ... I didn't lose ... it's a draw. Right, Ruby?" Fran gave her a quick wink and inhaled deeply again, trying to fill her aching lungs with air.

She smirked at Fran, "Just this once and only 'cause."

"'Cause why?" wondered Violet.

Ruby flicked her hand at Fran, "'Cause she's a self-centered, ugly old woman. That's why." Both Ruby and Fran burst into wild schoolgirl giggling.

Ruby stopped suddenly, looking directly into Fran's eyes, and quietly whispered, "Hush now or people will stare at us." With that, they roared even louder.

The other two ladies exchanged looks. Fran had left crying, and now she was laughing like a lunatic. It was Pearl who asked the question they were both thinking, "What's gotten into you two? You hide some hooch over there or somethin'?"

"No. Nothing but common sense." Ruby managed to get out through happy tears and cheeks that hurt from laughing.

"Yep, good old common sense," Fran gave Ruby a little hug, "From a good old friend." She wiped her eyes carefully trying not to disturb her mascara.

Ruby leaned in, to whisper into Fran's ear, "Did you see anybody laughing? Is anybody staring?"

She grinned back, "Yah, but they're all staring at you ... Funny Face!" Fran gave her a friendly poke in the ribs, making Ruby jump sideways with a sharp squeal.

Life on the Lawn

"Land sakes! Will you two settle down?" commanded Pearl. "You're acting downright silly. Now behave yourselves." She folded her arms tightly, signaling that she was dead serious and that she'd make a fuss if they didn't do as they were told. Mother Pearl had spoken.

Fran's straightened up her posture, regaining her customary ladylike composure.

"I'll get the lemonade I promised you. You girls want some too?" Violet and Pearl both nodded *Yes*. "Four lemonades, coming up." They watched her ringlets bounce as she left.

Fran cleared her throat, "So what did we miss?"

Violet instantly answered, "Nothing much." Pearl shifted her eyes away from Violet's, who was intently fidgeting with her bidding paddle, avoiding any kind of contact with Fran's eyes.

Fran's suspicious nature kicked in. Violet's response was offered up too fast for her liking. And why weren't they looking at her? They were holding something back, and she was damned well going to find out exactly what that was. Fran's face turned cold stone stern. "What happened? And tell me the truth. No bull flop, you hear me?"

Violet opened her mouth to say something, but Pearl broke in, "Are you asking about the Frenchman?"

Fran gave her a *what in the hell do you think I'm asking you about* look.

"Well, up until five minutes ago, he's been switching between mad as hell and downright miserable. But he's cheered up plenty now." Pearl pointed with her chin, "Take a look for yourself."

Violet squinted against the sunlight, "Yah, after you left, that idiot Virgil said something to him, and I guess that set him off. Heck! He was standing there writing in that little brown book of his, when all of a sudden, he whipped it on the ground and stomped his heel on it. And not just once either, but about six times. Got a few funny looks for it too."

Pearl budded in, "At that point, he started to head off in your direction when Emmett hollered at him to come back. 'Cause apparently he knew John-Paul was interested in the next lot that was up for bid. Stupid child, that Emmett boy."

Violet finished the story off, "It was the damnedest thing though. He just stood there for a time. You could see he was fighting against himself in his head. Then all of a sudden, he buckled, his body just collapsed. All down in the mouth, he was. He walked back and picked up his book. Dusted it off, stuck it in his shirt pocket and went back to bidding on the next lot. But he's been hot and cold the whole time since." She grinned up at her, "Well, that is until now."

Pearl joked, "And Fran ... has the back of your head caught on fire yet?"

"What? I mean, pardon?" Fran corrected herself.

Pearl looked over her shoulder, "The way he's staring at you, your head should burst into flames any second now."

An expression of terror washed across Fran's face, "So he is staring at me?"

"Yep," Violet confirmed it.

"Does he look mad?" Right there and then she couldn't decide herself whether she was still mad or plain hurt.

Pearl sized him up again, "Nooo … just kinda … apologetically love-sick."

Fran scrunched up her face, "That's not funny."

"Who's joking?" Pearl pointed with her nose, "Look for yourself."

Fran swallowed hard before turning around. Not to be obvious, she first watched Emmett who was yelling at Virgil about something silly. Then she casually glanced in John-Paul's direction. Pearl was right; he did look absolutely miserable. He was staring straight at her, making her thoughts swirl inside her head. She still didn't know how she felt about him or what he had done to her. But she was a proper lady, and her social standing required her to maintain her dignity and her pride. Taking a deep breath, she looked directly at him and gave him a pleasant southern smile. Instantly his face lit up, and he returned her smile, along with partial bow. Feeling her face flush pink, she turned her attention back to Emmett. Without moving her lips, she spoke softly to the others, "Girls? What's he doing now?"

Pearl played along with the game. She faced Violet, but looked passed her, "He's still watching you, and right now he seems pretty darned happy, He's smiling like a kid on Christmas mornin'."

Ruby interrupted by yelling, "Somebody want to give me some help here? Before I drop one of these." Fran spun around and ran to help her.

"Cold lemonade, just what I need." Violet dug into her side pack, "If I gotta take God damn bitter heart pills it might as well be with some fresh sweet lemonade."

"I got them. "Fran took two cups from Ruby's hands. She took a huge nervous gulp from one and handed the other one to Violet.

Ruby gave the other one to Pearl, "What's Emmett selling now?" All four ladies switched their attention to the auction while sipping on their cold drinks.

Virgil tugged the podium over the lumpy grass, stopping in front of the tall china cabinet. He mopped the sweat from his forehead, "This here a good spot, boss?" Emmett nodded his approval. For that, he was grateful. It was too heavy, and it was too hot for an old man like him to haul it all over the place. He managed another smile at Violet before being shooed away by Emmett. This time she sweetly waved back. His heart thumped, and his hands broke into a hot, clammy sweat. That was the exact moment he decided he'd finally ask her out on a date. He was in town for the next two days, and she was obviously interested. Yep, that was what he was going to do.

Ruby groaned, "That's an awfully big china cabinet. I wish I had the space for it at my place. It's beautiful." Fran and Pearl secretly grinned at each other but said nothing about their earlier conversation.

Life on the Lawn

Emmett plopped his dusty crumbled papers and gavel on top of the podium and climbed onto its platform. He eyed the crowd looking for potential bidders. Emmett had learned to study the crowd and pre-determine who the bidders for each individual lot might be. To his surprise, Jody Calfas was chomping at the bit on this lot. He studied him closely and wondered why a newly married man, living in a one bedroom apartment, would want such an oversized piece of furniture. Realizing it was none of his damned business *why*, he started that round of bidding. Clearing his parched raw throat, he announced the next lot for sale. He read the list description out loud, "Lu, Lu, Lot #42. One antique china cabinet. It's made of solid crosscut oak, and as you can see aged to perfection. Du, du, double-door upper and lower sections, plus two side-by-side drawers lined with deep blue velvet for your silverware. All glass and metal hardware are original and handcrafted. Opening bid will start at two-hundred-dollars with a reserve bid of three-hundred and fifty-dollars. Who'll start us off at two-hundred-dollars?"

Four signs shot up at the exact same instant. Emmett placed them in his memory for visual reference, John-Paul, Donald, Jody and of course, Bob Hawkins. Emmett's heart raced. What luck, four bidders - all with plenty of money to burn, precisely what he wanted. After all, the more money he made for his client, the greater his commission percentage would be in the end. And money was why he was there.

"O, O, Okay, one at a time boys." Using an old auctioneer's strategy, he accepted Jody's bid first, drawing him into the bidding battle at the get-go, in hopes it would hold him there longer, "Jody's got two-hundred-dollars. Do I hear two-hundred and twenty-five? I need two-hundred and twenty-five. Looking for ..."

Again, all four bidding paddles went up at one time.

Emmett laughed along with the other spectators. His father had trained him what to do in this type of situations. It was rare, but it happened. In the past, Emmett Sr. would've simply continued the bidding without accepting any one bid in particular. Eventually, the height of the bid would naturally eliminate those who couldn't afford it any longer. "O, O, Okay, okay." He calmed the crowd down with his hands, "I've got two-hundred and twenty-five. Do I hear two-fifty? I'm looking for two-fifty. Who'll give me two-hundred and fifty-dollars?"

The crowd roared again as each of the signs were hoisted into the air, one right after the other. All four men looked at each other as though they were surprised that the other was still bidding against them.

But it was John-Paul that got the most stares.

Emmett simply carried on as always, "Three-hundred? I'm looking for three-hundred? Three-hundred-dollars?"

Bob's paddle went up first, followed by John-Paul's, next was Jody's and finally was Donald's. This time the crowd only mildly chuckled. This odd phenomenon was creating a bewildering atmosphere for those within the congregation. As with most auctions, members of the crowd generally picked their favorite bidder and enjoyed rooting for them to win. But the multiple bidder situation had everyone a little unsure and quite confused as to who to choose.

"I have three-hundred. Do I hear three-fifty?" To save time, he jumped it up fifty-dollars this time, hoping to reduce it by one bidder, a lot faster. "Looking for three-hundred and fifty-dollars?"

Bob, Donald, and John-Paul raised their signs immediately. Emmett gave Jody time to think; it took him a few seconds before putting his sign up.

"Three-fifty. Do I hear four-hundred?"

Donald, Bob, and Jody, all raised their paddles at once, but this time John-Paul took his time.

Emmett asked him directly, "Monsieur, Four-hundred?"

To everyone's amazement, he shook his head *No* in reply. Straightening up from leaning on the fence, he coolly announced, "Six-hundred-dollars."

The crowd groaned. Bob's face went red while he closed his eyes in disbelief. The Frenchman had done it to him again, and his blood pressure was rising fast. Jody's body wilted with disappointment. Knowing he was out of the race, he glumly tossed his sign to the ground. Oddly, only Donald remained smiling.

Emmett pounded the gavel hard, in efforts to get everyone's attention. He then waited another few moments for them to settle down before starting again. The only ones left talking were Virgil and Betty, who were arguing about which was in the next lot to be auctioned off. It was Sammy that hushed them up with extra long Shhh ... that swished over his lips and passed by his slender finger in a way that made Virgil visibly uncomfortable. That made them both shut up.

Emmett had to rub it in, "Thank you, Sammy. Your auction etiquette is impeccable." It was a subtle dig that made Betty blush. Virgil was too busy being manly trying to counteract Sammy's embellished mannerisms, to really notice what Emmett had said. "Now, let's see the last bid was ... six-hundred-dollars.

Do I hear six-hundred and fifty-dollars?"

It was Bob's turn to throw in his sign. Both John Paul and Donald nodded their acceptance. Donald was still smiling. Emmett wondered how high he would go with his bid. "Six-hundred and fifty it is. Do I hear seven-hundred? I'm looking for seven-hundred." The audience was so silent, Emmett merely had to speak and everyone could hear him. The tension thickened and people clustered themselves closer together, allowing them to whisper without being heard by the others. No one wanted to miss a thing. Not a word or a movement.

Donald nodded and gave his sign a quick flick of the wrist. That motion made Virgil nervously shift on his feet. He knew if Donald won this bid, he'd have to deliver the cabinet to their house. He was not looking forward to being anywhere near that particular house. He didn't want Monsieur Bordeaux to win either, but it was better than go anywhere near those two 'peculiar' fellas.

John-Paul let a few moments go by before declaring, "Eight-hundred-dollars." This time he managed to pronounce the 'H' at the beginning of the word hundred.

All eyes focused on Donald. "Eight-hundred and fifty." He yelled it at Emmett. His expression showed both his desperation and his frustration at bidding against John-Paul and his endless amount of money.

Emmett didn't even say the name; he only pointed the gavel at John-Paul.

He leaned back against the fence, "One-thousand-dollars. And Monsieur Emmett, please call me by my main name – John-Paul, s'il vous plait."

Donald turned toward John-Paul to say something when Sammy stopped him. He placed his hand on his shoulder and loudly whispered. "We don't have room for it anyway. It's too big. We'll keep looking for one that's a better size."

But Sammy's consoling only irritated Donald further, "Shut up you ninny!" Everyone watched as Donald pushed Sammy aside and stomp off toward their farm. It was the whimpering Sammy chasing after him like a hen-pecked husband in tow that unnerved everyone. That site made the congregation whisper about other unpleasant confrontations they had witnessed between the two. A recent loud quarrel in the General Store, over which paint color to choose … cornflower blue or sage green. Donald won of course. Then Sammy had to return something he had bought without Donald being there. It wasn't what Donald approved of. And the worst was the time Donald out-and-out abandoned Sammy in town and drove home without him after one of their little disagreements.

Sheriff Morton gave him a ride back to their farmhouse. Everyone knew about it within days.

A hot, tired Emmett completed the bid. Hammering the gavel on the podium, he announced the final results of the bazaar multiple bidder war, "Lot #42 sold to Monsieur John-Paul Bordeaux at the cost of one-thousand-dollars."

The crowd murmured and milled about as Virgil carried over the next crate of items and slammed on the ground in front of the podium. As he walked away, he pointed to the box and hollered out to the crowd, "It's a box of Henry's old farm clothes. Why I bet, we get three or four hundred dollars for those." That made the crowd laughed, breaking the tension.

"Good one Virgil!" Violet yelled over the laughter. The others pretended that Violet hadn't been so common as to holler at the hired help. She opened her mouth to say something else, but Pearl loudly cleared her throat, implying that she should yell nothing further.

She crushed her paper cup, "Gee whiz, a girl can't have any kinda fun around you three." That's when she figured out that they didn't know about her and Virgil's flirting. And that was just fine with her. They'd only tease the daylights out of her anyway. And who needed that?

"That 'cause we're ladies. Not common alley cats." Frances bluntly stated, "Refined, proper ladies."

"Yes, it keeps us away from the rift-raft." Ruby secretly pointed toward the other side of the crowd, "You know. People like him."

"Oh, Lord Jesus, not him! I knew this day was going too good to last." Violet blurted out.

Pearl's face went pale at the sight of him, "Oh, hell! Not him! And not today of all days!"

"Is he still bothering you?" Ruby watched as her face went resolute, "He is, isn't he? What'd he do now?"

"Did he send you more flowers?" Fran's voice was half amusement and half repulsion.

"And chocolates," Pearl's rolled her eyes while her face flushed red.

"But didn't you tell him, you weren't interested?" Violet knew the answer, but she was enjoying rubbing it in.

"Yes!" Pearl snapped back, "But he's got in his head that he can woo me into going out with him. Personally, I wish he'd drop dead right there in that spot and leave me alone!"

"A dead man's body. Yah, that's just what this auction needs ... a little excitement." Fran joked by mimicking a huge yawn.

Ruby added her own sarcastic one-liner, "Yah, it's been sooo boring up until now."

"There's nothing funny at all about that man being here." She clenched her fists at her side, "I hope he stays over there and leaves me to hell alone." Now Pearl was getting concerned that other people would see him talking to her, even though she didn't want him to, and start to gossip about the two of them. Small town minds and mouths, could be cruel when they wanted to be.

"I hope he does. Come over here, that is." Fran smiled at Pearl, "I think the three of us could make it perfectly clear that you are not interested in him. Not one damned bit."

"I'm game." Violet rubbed her hands together, "I'm itchin' to tell somebody off, and right now Lester Wortman will do just fine."

That caught his attention. He heard someone say his name and turned to see who said it. His long, narrow face lit up when he spotted Pearl.

"Hell! Hell! Hell! Hell!" Pearl stepped behind Fran to hide, but it was no use, she was at least five inches taller than her and stuck out past her head. "Thanks a lot, Violet. Damn you!"

"Oops! Sorry Honey." Violet said it, but by the smile on her face, she really didn't mean it.

Ruby squealed, "Oh hell hounds! He's coming over here."

Lester Wortman was hard to miss, even in a crowd. He stood six foot five inches and weighed all of a hundred and thirty pounds. In his burgundy leisure suit with matching white belt and white paten loafers, he looked like a reject from a Retro 1980's Halloween party. He walked on stilt-like scrawny legs and his arms dangled awkwardly from his bony shoulders. A natural born oddball if there ever was one. Unfortunately, for Pearl, he was heading directly toward her.

He took off his white golf cap, exposing his overly greased black-dyed hair and smiled at her, "Miss Pearl." He bowed a slight greeting to the others, "Ladies."

Violet wasted absolutely no time. She wheeled her chair closer to him, "Lester Wortman what are you doing here?" Her finger was waggling furiously at him, "Didn't she tell you not to bother her anymore? And don't you be telling me no, 'cause I was there when she wrote the note."

"Yah, me too!" Ruby forced her fists on her hips as she glared up into his sunken skeletal face. She stepped to his left, turning him with her, "And I know what it read 'cause I helped her write it so you'd get the message loud and clear buster."

"Yah, me too!" echoed Fran from behind him. He had to turn right around to face her. "It was me who delivered it to you personally. And as you recall, I watched you read it!"

"So why are you here?" Violet poked him in the leg. She was sickened by the lack of flesh on his bones, the feel of it made her stomach churn.

At this point, he realized he was surrounded on all four sides by the women. Violet at the front in her wheelchair, Fran on his left, Ruby on his right and Pearl was standing behind him. He had a bad feeling about where he was presently standing. He immediately wished he was somewhere else — anywhere else — but right in the middle of those four riled up women.

Pearl tapped him on the shoulder to make him turn around to face her. She said the words hard, sharp and clear, "I done told you, I didn't want to date you. I done told you to stop callin' me. I done told you to leave me be. And I done told you to stop sending me things. Now I'm done being nice, the next time you bother me, I'll … I'll …" she grew overly angry and became so flustered she couldn't speak. The words whirled around in her head, but they wouldn't come out of her mouth.

Fran stepped between them and put her face right into his face, "She'll call me." She narrowed her eyes at him, "Do you want her to call me? Do ya, Lester? Do ya? Huh?" She had gotten so close; her nose almost touched the tip of his.

"No, Ma'am. Not you." He shook his head and tried to pull away from her. He took one step backward, stumbled and landed squarely in Violet's lap.

"Get off me ... you overgrown grease ball." She heaved him forward out of her lap making him ram into Fran, who automatically shoved him away, making him collide with Pearl.

Before Pearl could move, Ruby yelled, "Get away from her! Get! I said, get!" she started hitting him with Violet's apples. One after another, they stung his body as they hit him hard.

"Ouch!" He covered his face with his hands for protection, "Hey, stop it!" He pushed his hips out forward and tucked in his butt cheeks as the little hard apples stung his behind, "That hurts! Jesus, lady, cut it out!" Running away, he yelped behind him, "You ladies are cotton pickin' crazy!"

Emmett bellowed, "Ladies, is there a problem over there? Do you need any help?" Virgil stood on his tiptoes to see over the crowd. He had to make sure his Violet wasn't in trouble. He was prepared to rescue her if he had to. But he relaxed when he saw she was fine.

Pearl went crimson as Fran reassured him and everyone else who was watching, "Everything's fine Emmett Honey. We just had a little problem with a pest, but he's ... I mean, it's gone now." Pearl rolled her eyes in her head and turned even redder.

Emmett dismissively nodded and returned to the bidding.

All four of them straightened themselves up properly and acted as though nothing had happened. They nodded and smiled sweetly at those who were still staring; until everyone finally returned to watching Emmett.

With that Ruby announced, "We're alright, no body's talking. They're all listening to the sale."

Pearl let out a deep breath and turned to face her, "God damn it, Fran!"

"What did I do?" Fran didn't understand why Pearl was so mad and especially at her. "I was only trying to help."

Violet and Ruby knew what was coming next. Again, Ruby changed the subject back to the auction sale, "What's Emmett selling now?"

Violet helped her, "Damned if I know. I can't see a thing from down here. What's he selling Pearl?" Except that was the wrong person to ask.

"God damn it, Fran! How could you have done that?" Pearl's eyes were on fire.

Fran shrugged her shoulders, "What? Look, Emmett was about to cause a scene, I only nipped it in the bud."

"I'm not talking about that." She stepped closer to Fran, "Why'd you stick your nose in where it didn't belong?" Pearl jammed her finger into her chest, "It was my job to tell Lester off. It was my job to set him straight. It was my job to send him a running. Not

110

yours. God damn it, Fran." She abruptly turned about and groaned, "I'm getting some lemonade before I do something very unbecoming of a lady."

Fran went to follow her, but Ruby stopped her. Fran called after her, "Pearl, I only meant to help ..."

"She's upset, let her calm down first. Then you two can talk it out." Ruby rubbed the spot on Fran's arm where she had grabbed her maybe a little too tightly. "It'll be alright. You'll see."

Violet snickered loudly, "Hey, look, Emmett's sellin' Virginia's drawers."

They both asked it at the same time, "They're selling her underwear?"

"No, no, no." She waved away the ridiculous idea with her hand, "The chest of drawers from the big bedroom. You remember? The one with the six large drawers and the top two split in the middle."

"Oh yah, that one." Ruby pictured it in her head, "Doesn't it have carved ivory handles?"

That jogged Fran's memories, "And isn't there 'Mother of Pearl' inlay all through the top? That's a nice piece of furniture." She chuckled out, "I wonder how much John-Paul's going to pay for it."

Violet cocked an eye at them, "You girls remember the story behind this one?"

"Can't say that I do." Ruby stepped a little closer to Violet and knelt down beside her on the dried grass.

"Something about a doctor's wife, as I recall." Fran tapped her lip with her finger trying to remember. But the thought of Pearl being so angry with her kept popping into her head. "Um ... shouldn't we wait until

Pearl gets back?" Truth be told, Fran was worried about her — and their friendship.

"Nah, she knows all about it anyway. She was there when Henry brought it home from Charlotte. As it turns out, Henry went to Charlotte to pick up a tractor part that he couldn't find around here. It was planting time, and he needed it pronto. Planting waits for no one. You've got two weeks to plant your crops, or you're off schedule at the end of the season. And losing your crops to the rains can financially cripple a farm. So off to Charlotte went Henry."

Ruby inhaled a whistle, "Lordy, that's a long way to go for a single tractor part. Expensive trip too."

"Like I said, when you need a part, you need a part. Anyway, on his way into the city, he saw these men carrying furniture into this huge mansion. He noticed that one of the guys that was hauling in the furniture, was leaning on the truck, and holding on to his chest. Henry knew that man was in trouble by the paleness of his sweaty skin. He pulled his truck over, ran to the house and yelled for someone to fetch a doctor. You see, he didn't know it was actually a doctor's house in the first place. The doctor came a runnin' and helped Henry get him into his car. Later, Henry got a letter from the Governor telling him how brave he was. Said, he was an American hero and how he should be proud of himself for helping out a stranger. City folk! They think that doing something neighborly like that is something ... extraordinary. Pitiful ain't it? You gotta feel sorry for those 'frightened of the consequences' city people?"

"Good Lord! Get back to the dresser, will yah." Fran hated it when Violet rambled on about other facts in a story that, in reality, weren't part of the story at all.

"Oh yah, where was I? So that meant they were short one mover and they had to have the truck unloaded and returned that day. Henry offered to help out, for money of course. When the last of the boxes were put in the kitchen, the doctor's wife came storming in, screaming and all upset. After a few words with the housekeeper, it was decided that the one dresser would have to be thrown out. It didn't match the rest of the furniture in the master bedroom. When Henry realized which dresser they were talking about, he offered to take it off their hands instead of being paid cash. She agreed to the deal and Henry brought it home to Virginia as a gift. She loved it. Well except for the funny smell."

Ruby stood up, dusted off her knees and enquired, "Funny smell?"

"It had a funny smell that Virginia couldn't get rid of. She said it smelled of fancy French perfume. She always joked that it smelled of *the cheap harlots of Charlotte*. She tried everything to get it out. Bleach, vinegar, baking soda, heck, even ammonia wouldn't touch it." Violet laughed to herself, "Personally, I think Henry like the smell of it on Virginia's clothes. You see, Virginia kept her fancier clothes in that dresser and whenever they went somewhere elegant ... well let's just say Virginia told me he usually got pretty frisky when they got home. Old dog!"

"Henry? Our Henry?" Fran seemed astonished that mild and obedient Henry could get sexually aroused over a something as simple as a fragrance. "No. I don't believe it. Not of him. He's too reserved for that sort of thing."

"Lord Franny, first of all, he is a man. They get excited over just about anything. And secondly, a scent is a powerful thing. Trust me on that fact." Her eyes lit up and a sinful grin swept across Violet's lips.

Pearl bent down to her level and pointed to her mouth, "And what's that all about? Do tell us, Miss Violet?"

"You're back! I'm sorry. Really, I am. You can yell at me some more if it will make you feel better." Fran was practically begging her, "Please yell at me?"

"I'm not that mad, but you shouldn't have got in my way. It was my job to tell him that just because we are both tall, doesn't mean that we are meant to be together for the rest of eternity."

"You're kidding? He said that?" Ruby's ringlet shook as she shivered in disgust.

"Yes. And I was the one that needed to say that I don't like being called his African Aphrodite."

"Oh! Yuk!" Fran nearly gagged at the idea of creepy Lester calling her that name. Mainly, having him call Pearl any type of romantic name, made her skin crawl.

"Yah, makes me want to retch up just saying it out loud," she covered her mouth with her hand.

"Oh, I get it now. A Black Goddess of love. You know it's kinda sweet in a way?" Both Pearl and Fran shot Ruby a shut-up look. She insisted, "Well it is?"

"Anyway, it was my place to insist that he leave me alone. And if he didn't stop, I would be forced to talk to Sheriff Morton and press charges against him." Even though she kept her voice low, Pearl's face was filled with resentment, "And that, Fran, was my one and only chance to say it to his face." Once again, she stabbed her pointed finger at Fran, then turned into her own chest, "And because of you, I didn't get to say it!"

Now Fran understood what she had done wrong.

She felt terrible. Tears filled her eyes as she said it one more time, "I'm really sorry. I only meant to help."

Pearl crossed her arms and chastised her, "Next time, just shut the hell up and let me speak for myself." Even though she was furious with Fran, she couldn't stand it. It was difficult to watch a friend fall apart and cry from guilt. Especially since that friend was sincere about looking out for her best interests. "Okay?" She fished out a tissue of her pocket and handed it to Fran, "Oh here, take this."

"Okay." Fran noisily blew her nose, "Shut up and let you speak. Got it."

There stood in an awkward silence until Ruby began to giggle, "African Aphrodite? Lord loving Jesus, now I've heard it all."

Violet cracked up next. In between snorts of laughter, she held out her hand, "Give me one of those. I think I'm gonna need it."

Pearl handed Violet and Ruby a tissue each, then took one for herself. "You think you're laughing? You had to hear my sister Opal. I'm sure she musta peed in her pants before I kicked her out of my house." She shook her head at the absurdness of the situation. Then, knowing it would get the girl going, she poked fun at herself, "African Aphrodite? A Dark Princess, maybe? But definitely not a Black Goddess."

Those words sent them into wholehearted hysterics. Fran bent over with the pain in her belly from laughing too hard. First, she had cried, and then she laughed. She thought to herself, *Isn't it grand to have friends that ride the emotional roller coaster along with you.*

"Shh ... Emmett's looking at us again. Settle down.

Hush up now." Pearl didn't want a repeat performance. "I mean it ... Shut up!" Ruby had to walk away from them before she totally fell apart. "Besides, do you want John-Paul to think you're an immature idiot? 'Cause right now he's watching us pretty close. Well, actually, he's gawkin' at you Franny."

With that, Fran took control of her childish behavior and transformed herself into the fine Southern Bell she strived to be at all time — and sometimes — at all costs. "He's watching me again?" She straightened her blouse's buttons, and finger combed her braid end again. Unconsciously her hips swayed back and forth with the excitement of being admired from such a distance and by such a handsome man. She inhaled the memory of that precise thrilling moment, capturing it forever in her mind and deep in her heart. These delicious emotions, she of course, kept to herself.

"Honey, he never stopped." Violet poked her in the leg, "And you should go over there and talk to him." She shoved the back of her leg, "Go on."

Fran swatted behind her, slapping Violet's hand away, "You know I can't do that," she whimpered. She clasped her hands together in an awkward attempt to find a place for them to be, instead of excitedly flailing about. In her mind, it allowed her the appearance of self-restraint.

"Why not?" Violet looked up at her and set her eyes directly on Fran's, "You ain't getting any younger, you know. Get it while you still can." She dropped her eyes, "I know I wish I still could." She knew that last comment would knock some sense into her friend.

She took a step forward but stopped. John-Paul wasn't watching her any longer; he was concentrating on the next item up for bid. She tried to brush it off by adding an abrupt, "Later."

"What? Why?" She hit the arm of her chair, "Why not now, damn it?

"Because right now I think he's more interested in buying that smelly old dresser than talking to me." Turning her head, she widened her eyes at Pearl, pleading with her to change the subject and fast.

Pearl nodded slightly in sympathy, "Yah and besides right now, she's gotta help me pick up your apples." She bent over to pick one up and bounced it her hand, "I can't believe Ruby threw these at him?' Pearl face turned mean, "Damn him! I hope they hurt like hell too!"

With a quick glance, Fran checked to see if indeed John-Paul was still staring. He was. "Let me help you." She positioned herself to where she could make the most impact and be able to watch its results. She slowly leaned forward to pick up an apple, rounding her behind just so, while curving her back and sticking out her round breasts all at the exact same time. She allowed herself a fleeting look in his direction. She giggled, "Mission accomplished." She witnessed his mouth dropped open as he half straightened up in her direction. She grinned secretly to herself, *You still got it girl. Time to go get him.*

From the podium, she heard Emmett calling, "John Paul? Are you in or out?"

John-Paul broke away from her and closed his mouth. He switched his attention back to Emmett, "Pardon, I am sorry Emmett. Where are we in the dollars?"

"Bob's at two-hundred and seventy-five. You bidding three-hundred?" It was a dumb question, yet Emmett had to ask it.

"Oh yes, Three-hundred." He sent a smile to Fran and waited for a reply. She obliged him with an innocent, but seductive smile that she hoped he'd translated into *Come get me!* That made his green eyes light up, and his mouth go dry as he swallowed hard. Now confident that she had him right where she wanted him, she broke the connection and focussed back on Emmett.

"I've got three-hundred. Do I hear three-fifty? I'm looking for three-fifty?" Emmett pointed at Bob.

His sign waved slightly. He knew there was no point in getting excited about it. John-Paul would outbid anything he could possibly bid with or afford. Now he was raising the price so Emmett could make more commissions off John-Paul's endless supply of money. If he couldn't win, Emmett should.

Emmett was tired, and the dry air was hurting his throat. He directly asked John-Paul, "Four-hundred?" He nodded in agreement. The sound of a car on gravel was faintly heard in the background, and a sparse plume of dust drifted across the open field.

Emmett was taking a drink of water, "Bob, four-fifty?"

Bob winked at him, "Nope. Let's make it six-hundred."

Emmett swallowed hard. Bob was fixing the sale. Something he positively didn't want. It went against his own ethics to cheat anyone, even those who obviously had more money than brains. But what really concerned him was, if he and Bob were caught by the Authorities, it would cost Emmett his Auctioneers License. Emmett nervously cleared his throat, "Six-hundred it is." In his head, he was hoping John-Paul would decline the next bid and stick Bob with an old dresser for six-hundred. That would teach Bob a lesson — a very costly lesson. "I'm looking for six-fifty?" Again, he looked straight at John-Paul.

At the beginning of his career, John-Paul had been taken a few times by unscrupulous auctioneers before learning to recognize the facial expressions that were exchanged between scoundrels. Reading the face of Emmett and then Bob's, he determined this was not the case at this auction. Bob was the rabble-rouser, and Emmett clearly wanted no part of it. He did decide to have a little fun with Bob. He too winked at Emmett and yelled out, "No." Emmett caught the wink and sent a quick nod agreeing that he'd go along with his gag. Emmett said nothing — he neither confirmed nor denied Bob's six-hundred-dollar bid. He merely prolonged time by shuffling his papers; checking off this and that; pretending to search for some fictitious information and the whole while fighting back a mischievous grin.

Bob spun around to look at John-Paul. Then back to Emmett. Panic set in his eyes. He looked back at John Paul and then back to Emmett. Now he was getting worried. His feet danced in a tight circle on the dry grass. His head started to hurt. Once again back to John Paul and then to Emmett. His mind whirled with questions. Where in the hell was he going get six-hundred-dollars? And for a dresser he didn't even want! He pulled a hanky from his back pocket and wiped his sweat-beaded face. Six-hundred-dollars? Suddenly, he didn't feel so good. His stomach started to churn wildly; he thought he was going to either throw up or faint.

Seeing the color drain from his face, John-Paul decided Bob had endured enough and loudly cleared his throat. Emmett took the signal, "Oh, sorry there folks, I had to find something. Numbers mostly. Paperwork's such a pain in the-you-know-what." He cleared his throat — twice, drawing time out a wee bit longer. He was savoring every second of it. Bob had done him wrong and needed to be taught to never toy with another person's moral values. "Now, where were we?" Trying not to smile too much, he continued, "Oh yes, John-Paul said no, so Bob your bid ..."

Right on the mark, John-Paul chimed in, "I said 'no' to six-'undred and fifty ..." Much to Emmett's amusement he paused, also stretching it out even further, "but I will bid seven-hundred."

Bob nearly collapsed from relief; his frazzled body wilted in spot. With his hands on his knees to prop himself up, he yelled, "He can have it." He turned to face John-Paul, "Frenchy fella, it's all yours." He hoisted his hand up in the air and shook his head at Emmett, "And Buddy, I am done for the day." That made Emmett smirk, "Are you sure Bob? There's only one item left. And it's a heavenly thing to own, even for you Bob." He knew his friend was a creature of curiosity and he loved tormenting him with that fact. Emmett waved a sheet of paper at him, "You don't want to miss this one? Why, it would be almost sacrilege if you did. You just gotta stay. If you don't, you'll regret it Bob."

In an instant, his got-to-know mentality got the better of him. He couldn't help himself, "Yah. What is it?"

Emmett made him wait.

Chapter Five

Emmett shuffled his papers about, put his initials here and there, delaying time as he did before, making Bob wait. He crossed out numbers, then replaced them with other ones. He tallied the totals and shook his head in imaginary disbelief. To kill even more time — and to drive Bob slowly crazy — he called Virgil over to deliver one of the wrinkled blue forms to Betty for verification of a final selling price. He kept an eye on Bob to see how excited and how annoyed he was becoming. His buddy was tilting his head to the right with one eye partly closed. He had his hands shoved deep down into his pockets. And every now and then, he'd sweep the toe of his boot in front of him, making a big arcing line through the dirt. Then he'd stomp his feet together under himself. Emmett thought back to the days when Bob had to wait outside the house while Emmette finished his chores. Emmett smiled at the childhood memories and that vision before him. Things hadn't changed much over the years. Bob was basically still that same little impatient boy who didn't like to wait for the fun to start. Today was no different.

He was drawing out time to aggravate Bob, and it was working beautifully.

The four ladies watched Emmett while he waited for Virgil to return with the form. Violet broke their silence, "You know. I always detested auction sales. They're so ... so ... damned discouraging."

"Why's that?" Pearl wondered what her reasons were. Her own reasons were family related. Slavery and auctions had a long ugly history together.

"Well think about it? You're born and then get bigger and next you go to school. The next thing you know, you're all grown up and working. Then, if you're lucky, you meet someone nice and get married. You buy a house and have some children. Time goes by, and before you know it, the children are married and gone, living their own lives. You get older, whether you want to or not. Soon you can't take care of yourself while living alone in your own home. So, there you are, standing there, holding onto two suitcases with all your belongings that they'll allow you to take to the nursing home. And spread out before you, is all your other belongings ... your life on the lawn ... for everyone to scrutinize and buy at for-next-to-nothing. She let out a heavy melancholy sigh, "The memories of those things don't count one damned bit, only what they're worth dollar wise." She shook her head in disappointment, "Makes me wanna sell all my valuables right now! Today! So, I can enjoy now what the sale money would have brought me later on. Heck, maybe a trip to England. Oh! No! Wait ... Paris, France!

Yah ... Paris. Oh ... Paris in the spring." A romantic smile swept across her face, "Mmm ... I'd like that.

Who wants to come with me on a French adventure?"

Fran's eyes twinkled sinfully as she ogled John-Paul's tall, lean body, "Right now, I'm thinking about my own type of French adventure."

"I think, he's thinking the same thing. You gonna talk to him soon? Chances are he'll be leaving right after the auction, and you may never see him again." Ruby's voice taunted her, hopefully pushing her to talk to him.

"I'm thinking about it." She tapped her finger contemplatively on her lips.

Pearl smiled sweetly at her, "Well don't think too long, this is the last item up for bid. Take the chance, Franny. I've got a good feeling about this one."

"Shh. Here comes Virgil." Violet leaned forward in her chair to hear things better and get a closer look at Virgil. The other ladies exchanged favorable looks. They all thought it was time Violet had a little romantic courtship of her own. As if on cue, Virgil sent a smile their way. Violet blushed and sent him one back.

Virgil handed the form back to Emmett. After shuffling his papers one more minute, he cleared his throat, "The fu, fu, final sale of today's auction is ... well, it's a crying shame, tu, tu, that's what it is." He held it high into the air, a black leather bound Bible. "One family bible." His arm wavered under its massive weight, "This Bible contains the records of nine generations of the Phillips' family. Hand scribed with illustrations in full color." He lowered his voice slightly and spoke to the people at the front of the crowd, "Why the kids didn't want it, is beyond me? It would've been nice if they would have kept it and passed it on down to generation number ten. It always amazes me that Henry and Virginia raised such selfish money hungry children. You just never know do ya?" People in the crowd nodded in agreement. He cleared his sore throat signifying the end of his lecture. "Anyway, we'll be starting the bid at one-hundred-dollars. Do I hear one-hundred-dollars?"

No one budged. Bob shoved his hands deeper into his pockets and shook his head *No* but mostly it illustrated his disgust for the whole situation.

"Come on folks. I mean this is the first time I've seen a bible not bring in money. Is anyone bidding? Anyone?"

Some people folded their arms tight, while others made the sign of the cross, hoping in some way to eradicating the unpleasant act of disgracing a family's Holy Bible.

Emmett turned his focus to the one person who had been bidding on everything, "Monsieur John-Paul, are you interested in bidding on this item?" At that very moment, something caught his attention. There was someone standing in the opening of the Phillips' kitchen back door. With his hand, he shadowed his eyes against the bright sunlight. It was Katie, Virginia, and Henry's daughter. Knowing what he had just said about her and her brother, he dipped his head in apologies. Without hesitation, she accepted it with a kind wave and stepped out onto the back path. Emmett found himself with no words. He couldn't believe that she would have enough nerve to attend the very auction her husband, her brother and herself had neglected to acknowledge. Nor did they bother to visit their ailing father.

As others noticed his stunned stillness, they followed his stare, tracing it back to Katie. She held a friendly smile on her face as she nodded greetings to those she knew from her younger years of living on the farm. The midday breeze blowing through the leaves was the only sound that could be heard over the crowd's silence as she made her way to where John-Paul stood. He greeted her with the traditional French style double cheek kiss followed by a firm handshake. That sent a massive ripple of murmurs and finger pointing throughout the congregation.

Katie stood proudly beside John-Paul, and with all the dignity she could gather, she calmly turned to face the gawking crowd. After a deep breath and a squeeze of John-Paul's hand, her timid voice boomed over their muttering, "Please Emmett, continue."

"Um ... yes ... um. Monsieur John-Paul, do you wish to bid on this Bible?" He laid his hand on its top, making him feel oddly uncomfortable, a sense of truth and honesty nagged at his soul.

Katie smiled up at John-Paul and nodded, "Do it."

"You are sure, Madame?" he looked directly into her blue eyes. She simply nodded her absolute approval. John-Paul placed his hand on her tiny shoulder, faced Emmett and boldly announced, "Two-thousand-dollars."

A different kind of smile swept across Katie's face. Innocents mixed with revenge and satisfaction.

The crowd's whispering and mumbling were deafening compared to its earlier silence. Words like madwoman, lunatic, and cahoots could be heard above the murmuring hum. Groups of people began to shift, forming little clusters. Some took sides with Katie, praising her for returning to her childhood farm. Others condemned her for no longer being part of her father's life. But no one could understand why she was standing with the French outsider. Who was he to her and why did she give him the order to 'do it'?

Emmett felt the tension building within the crowd and decided to promptly finish the sale so that everyone would leave before trouble broke out. "Today's final item, sold to Monsieur John-Paul for two-thousand-dollars." He smashed the gavel hard making its loud crack echo through the thick humid air. "And that cu ... cu ... concludes the auction of Mr. Henry Phillips and his late wife, Virginia." He slapped his ledger closed and gathered up the remaining papers. "Au, au, all those needing to pay for items, please see Betty for payment and pick up. If you need your items delivered, you see Virgil, and he'll get the details of where and when. Thu, thu, thank you for coming out today and please drive home carefully. Remember, you're all going to be leaving at once, so be patient with each other." He hoped they would take his suggestion and leave promptly, but unfortunately, no one budged. Instead, they stood in place, watching, whispering, and waiting — waiting for an explanation.

Life on the Lawn

They watched John-Paul open his brown leather journal, laying it out flat to show Katie the figures. They spoke French, irritating those who were close enough to hear their conversation, since they couldn't understand the foreign language, therefore had no idea what they were saying to each other. At the end of the discussion, John-Paul pointed at the stack of crates and held up one finger as if requesting something specific out of the massive pile. In the manner his hands were flailing about, he was obviously explaining something significant to Katie. An enormous smile spread across her pale face and whole-heartedly nodded in agreement. She glanced in the direction of the four ladies and covered a giggle with her hand.

He guided her attention back to his journal. After a little more discussion and hand waving, they both seemed satisfied with the final total, and a shake of hands sealed the deal. With things settled, Katie pulled a chequebook from her tiny handbag. Carefully balancing it on the fence, she wrote out a cheque and handed it to John-Paul. He checked the total against his leather ledger while Katie continued to write another cheque. She presented it to him with tiny curtsy. He read the cheque, folded it in half and tucked into his shirt pocket, then comically patting it in place along with rocking on his heels. The both laughed at his silliness before they shook hands and exchanged another French-style kiss. As John-Paul escorted Katie to the registry table, they continued to casually chit-chat in his foreign tongue. The onlookers watched in amazement at the sight – their little Katie Phillips effortlessly speaking French and John-Paul carrying her cheque in his hand. Speculation raced through the crowd, yet no one knew the answers. Betty was all smiles when John-Paul submitted the cheque to her. As predicted, Betty had the figures itemized and totaled. Checking his numbers against hers, she accepted the cheque and stamped the tally sheet 'PAID IN FULL.' She hesitated for a few moments, unsure which to give the paper to. Finally, she simply offered it to the air between them, letting them decide who should take it. Katie was the one who took the paper and folded it carefully into quarters before slipping it into her small handbag. "Oh, and Betty, would you please ask Emmett to deposit that cheque as soon as possible? It would sure make my life easier." Betty nodded that she would.

That made the staring spectators start up again. It was Bob who asked what they were all thinking. He shoved his way to the front, "Now just a damned minute! What the hell's going on here?"

Emmett smelled trouble — big trouble, "Bob. You be civil now. Ru, ru, remember who she is."

"Oh, I remember all right." He crossed his arms and narrowed his eyes at her, "Why are you here? And why now? You didn't want anything to do with this auction two months ago when Emmett tried to contact you in New York. Did ya? And yet here you are handing out cheques to a French fella. What gives Katie-Kins?" That had been his pet name for her in high school. He hated to admit it to himself, but he still had a soft spot for her in his heart. He'd talk to her about that matter later, but right now, he wanted answers.

Life on the Lawn

John-Paul started to defend her, but Katie broke in with a halting hand, "I'll answer him. This is my mess, not yours." She turned away from John-Paul, "You're absolutely right. In a way, I am guilty of not caring about my father or this farm. That was until two weeks ago." Her face flushed pink, yet she held her head high as she talked directly to those she knew in the crowd. "You see up until two weeks ago I had no knowledge that this auction even existed. And if it wasn't for my friend John-Paul here, I would have never known at all." Ashamed of her current situation, she lowered her head and studied her feet before continuing. "Many of you know that my husband, Richard, is not the kindest man in my life. Well, as it turns out, he's meaner than you or I could have ever suspected. When Emmett sent notices of my father's auction, Richard hid them from me. When it comes to me, he has a habit of censoring all the information I receive from the outside world." She swallowed down her tarnished pride.

She faced Emmett and spoke directly to him, "I didn't return your calls because I didn't know they ever existed. He concealed those from me too. Be assured, if I had known that this auction was taking place, I would have stopped this whole thing from happening the second I found out. I'd like to apologize for what that rotten bastard husband of mine has done." She swallowed hard but said it out loud for all to hear, "Richard is a nasty, spiteful man. It was a mistake to marry him."

John-Paul rubbed her back gently, "You must tell them the rest."

She dug into her handbag, "Actually folks, you know those two cheques I just wrote, well they're from his bank account, and once they've all cleared, I'm giving him these." She confidently waved the tightly folded blue-wrapped bundle of papers in the air, "Divorce papers. I had them drawn up on the very same day John-Paul told me about a 'Notice of Auction.' You see, although he receives hundreds of notices at his antique shop, this one in particular caught his attention. It was the address that stuck out in his mind. He knew I came from this part of the country and wondered if I had ever heard of a town called Olive Grove. He also wanted to know if it would be worth him traveling here for this auction and what the possibility of high-quality antiques would be. When he mentioned Olive Grove, it made me curious, but when he told me the exact address, I couldn't believe it. It was my Daddy's house and my family's things that were up for sale. At first, I was furious. I wondered why no one from back home had contacted me. Then I realized why. The why, was Richard. After a thorough search of his law office, I found inner office memos and the many notices that the Sigmon and Son Co. had sent regarding this auction. And let me tell you, it made my blood boil. He had gone too far this time, and that's when I called John-Paul." She smiled up at him. "He had a plan in place in no time."

"Anyt'ing for you Katie." Realizing that sounds too attentive and somewhat affectionate, he hastily corrected it by adding, "Friends should always be t'ere for friends, no?" He glanced at Fran just to be sure the message got through to her. He relaxed when Fran batted her eyes and smiled back.

"We worked quickly, arranging things in ways that wouldn't alert anyone ... especially Richard. You see, if he or Thomas discovered what I was about to do, they would have made my life pure hell." Several of the ladies who knew details of Katie's miserable marriage, shuffled, and twisted with understanding and sympathy.

John-Paul explained his part, "That is why I came ahead of time. To study the area, its persons and my ... um ... competition. I too, do not like this Richard and wish our Katie to be rid of him." He tapped her on the shoulder, "May I tell them?" She nodded in agreement. In a loud baritone voice, he announced, "She is not only my great friend; she will now be my business partner. She will manage our shop. T'is will free me to travel for auctions all over the country. She 'as a brilliant mind for antiques and now I see why ... she grew up surrounded by them." He gestured with his hand at the string of furniture and stack of crates.

Katie sent Bob a delicate smile, "Please forgive John-Paul and myself for our deception. Please understand that my intentions come from my heart. The money that Richard will pay for my heirlooms will finance my father's staying at home." Several faces in the crowd lit up with surprise. "Yes, that's right, as of tomorrow my father will be living here again. I've arranged for Eliza Woodman to be his live-in homecare nurse so he can stay right here on the farm where he belongs." Tears filled her eyes, "I owe him that much ... and a whole lot more." She inhaled deep to ease the lump in her throat, "To all those who purchased any of today's items, I offer you three times what you paid for them. I wish to return my Daddy's things back to him." She couldn't hold it back any longer; her heart choked her words. She closed her eyes to stop the tears, but they streamed down her cheeks nonetheless.

Bob stepped forward, putting his arms around her, "Katie-Girl, you can have the things back ... no extra charge." The whispering started all over again.

That made her stop crying, "No three times the price. Richard needs to pay for what they've done to my Daddy and me. And since money is the only thing he really gives a damn about, that's where I'll get him ... right in the wallet. By the way, Thomas is next in line. And I know just how to make him squirm for his part in this."

John-Paul grinned in agreement, "We shall make him suffer."

Hardness washed over her face, "You see my darling big brother has been manipulating his clients. Thomas takes their hard-earned money, promising to pay the I. R. S. with it on their behalf. But instead, he stockpiles the paperwork and places their money in his own personal bank account, which he spends from freely. He replenished it with each newly milked client; keeping a constant cycle of client's money. Later ... generally seven months later ... those clients receive written notification from the government asking why they have neglected to file their papers and why they haven't paid their current taxes. That's when they call his firm wanting answers as to why. Thomas uses his charms and powers of persuasion to reassure them that there must have been an error on the part of the I.R.S. and that he would have it all straightened out in no time." She had been talking so rapidly, she had to take an extra deep breath before continuing, "He takes money ... clients money ... from his own personal account to cover the taxes they owed, finally files the paperwork that should have been filed with the government months before. Eventually, all is amended. And many of his clients consider him to be their white knight against the evil I.R.S. To his clients, it seems on the up and up. They never questioned a thing. Well, I asked. I asked John-Paul's lawyer and a Federal I.R.S. agent. And the question I asked was ... is this legal?" Her hands formed tight fists at her side while her face scowled solidly with the allegation.

John-Paul rubbed her back, "Katie, you must stop t'is. You know how t'is upsets you so." His expression showed his true concern for her. This was more than a business partnership, but one of respect and pure fondness for a friend.

From the rear of the crowd, an elderly male voice called out, "Katie is that you? Where are you Honey?" The people in the crowd stepped aside, creating a clear corridor that revealed Henry Phillips. He stood with his hand shading his old eyes and searched for his daughter. Finally spotting her, he coaxed her closer with a wave, "Katie? Come here Kitty Kat. Let me see ya!"

Like a little child, Katie ran to her father, hugging him close, she whispered, "Welcome home Daddy." They held each other tight at the waist as only a father and daughter could. Walking toward the house, everyone smiled to hear her say, "You must be tired from your trip? Let's go inside and get you settled in. I brought some ice tea - extra strong with lots of lemon, just the way Mama use to make it." Their voices faded when the back door closed behind them.

Hoping not to cry in front of everyone, Emmett drew a deep, jagged breath. He gathered himself together and announced, "Thu, thu, that concludes today's events. Please, folks, let's clear out of here so they can get on with things. Come on, let's go." He shooed them along with his hands, "Go on. Go home and get out of this hellish heat."

Slowly the horde drifted away. Small clusters of people climbed into cars and farm trucks, eventually disappearing down the driveway, leaving plumes of summer dust behind them.

Secretly, John-Paul had kept an eye on Fran's movements. He didn't want her to go before he had a chance to talk to her again. Noticing that she was preparing to leave with her friends, he knew he had to move fast before she left. He hurried over to the stack of crates that were in his section. He moved this one and that one, searching for the exact crate. "Ah, t'ere you are," he muttered to himself, "Come with me, you little trouble maker." He turned in time to see the four ladies head down toward the path. He shouted to them, "Mademoiselle Frances! Wait! Wait! I wish to speak to you. Please wait?"

Life on the Lawn

The others slowed down as Fran stopped to wait for him. As good friends do, they walked ahead of them, leaving enough distance for privacy, but close enough for protection if needed.

John-Paul caught up to her, "Mademoiselle Frances before you depart, I wish to give you t'is gift. Please allow me to give t'is?" In his hand, he held Virginia's red cookbook. "Please take t'is as a gift from me? It would please me if you could keep your friend's memories." He slid it towards her, "Please accept it?" The expression on his face was a mixture of pleading and apology. If she didn't accept it, he was convinced his heart would shatter.

Fran was taken aback by his offering, "I ... I ..."

He took hold of her wrist, turned her palm upward, and gently placed the book in her hand. "But before you take t'is gift; please tell me why t'is book is more important than the others? I too am ... what was that word?" The frustration of translating French words to English in his head showed on his face.

"Sentimental?"

"Oui, sentimental! I believe that is why I am in the antique business. Everything holds the memories and secrets of the people who owned them. Each one has a story locked inside." He flashed his green eyes at her, "I would enjoy knowing about t'is cookbook's story."

She managed to collect her scattered thoughts, "Like I said before, it's really a long story, and I don't wish to bore you with it."

"Nonsense, I would love to 'ear about t'is story. Maybe you could tell me t'is story over dinner. Per'aps t'is evening?" He fluttered his eyes at her.

His eyes paralyzed her. Again, they made it impossible for her to think. Her mind was swirling like a tornado. Her knees went weak, and she braced them against each other, so she didn't slide down to the ground. Her heart pounded so hard in her ears all she could manage was a nodded, Yes.

"Magnifique! I will come to you at seven o'clock. Yes?" He asked in that odd broken French manner which confused her at first.

She began to step away — to escape the connection with his powerful hypnotizing eyes, "Oh. Yes. That would be lovely. I live at ..."

He stopped her in mid-sentence, "I know where you live. I will not be late. Au revoir Mademoiselle Frances. Until tonight." With that, he promptly turned on his heels and headed for Virgil who was helping Bob bring the Phillips' belongings back into the farmhouse.

Fran stood in spot, staring after him. Her head stopped whirling long enough for her to enjoy the sight of John-Paul's tall, lean body lifting boxes and carrying them into the kitchen.

Ruby went to get Fran, "I should get her. We need to get going."

Pearl stopped her with an outstretched arm across the chest, "Not just yet."

"What? Why not?" Ruby was clueless as always.

"Lord Ruby! Look at her! Don't you think Franny's kinda lost in John-Paul right now? We can wait."

She shrugged her shoulders, "Well, I guess we could wait a little longer."

"Ruby Carson, has it been so long ago that you can't spot the sparks of passion starting to ignite?" Violet scolded.

"I guess it has been a while," She lamented, "Damned near a year." She paused to test if either one of them took notice of what she had said.

Pearl caught it, "A year? But Vernon's been gone for over ten years. That means you've ...? Details, we want details."

Violet urged, "Spill it girl."

Ruby blushed and beamed like a schoolgirl, "Do you remember the wine salesman from up north that was staying at the Inn?"

"Yah," Violet said it more as a question than as an answer.

"His name was Oscar. Wasn't it?" Pearl added it with a shocked expression. She couldn't picture it in her mind. Little pudgy Ruby and that tall, tanned Oscar. A highly unlike match — especially in the boudoir. She needed to be sure, "Oscar, the cute fella that's a salesman for Tippin's Winery's?"

Violet purred, "The man with the square shoulders and delightfully round behind? Oh, that bum! It was the perfect size for squeezin' by the handful." She cupped at the air mimicking the action of embracing his bottom, "He was all jammed into those taut black dress trousers and topped off by that deep red polo shirt."

"Yep, that Oscar." She confirmed proudly. Once her curls stopped bouncing, she continued, "Well, you know I visit Shirley's Inn a couple of times a week. Well, the one night he was there on the front veranda with her. They were talking and sampling one of the bottles of wine that he was peddling. When I showed up unexpected like, they opened another bottle of a different kind, and when that one was empty, he opened another bottle. Oh, girls, the three of us must've drunk eight or nine bottles of wine that night. And not small ones. Those huuuuuuge ones." She fanned her face with her hand, "Now you know me and wine? Gets me downright loose, randy and reckless. I evidently started flirtin' with Oscar, and he flirted right back. I couldn't help it." She closed her eyes, remembering the moment, "The night was so warm, and the soft breezes was filled with the cool, sweet scent of summer clover. It made me feel like I was in senior high again. Shirley, God bless her soul, surmised that I was too intoxicated to walk home and simply suggested that I spend the night in one of her empty rooms. Oscar quickly agreed with her and opened another bottle of merlot. That last one sent me over the top." Her arms swayed in mid-air, "It was well after 2 a.m. when we floated to our rooms. Shirley said Goodnight to Oscar and me, then disappeared into her quarters. That left me and Oscar walking up the stairs to our rooms ... alone together. When I reached my door, I turned to say Goodnight to him, and he really stepped in close to me and whispered 'May I smell your hair Miss Ruby?' Before I could answer, he had his face buried in my hair ... right beside my damned ear! And you know what that can do to a girl? He started stroking my hair, and my head started whirling about. Oh Lord, those thick, strong hands were gently stroking my head. My knees kinda melted and I lost all common sense. And when he took my face in both his hands and planted a kiss on me ...

girls I was a goner. Those lips of his were so sweet and soft. I'd never kissed lips that soft." She shrugged her shoulders, "And that was that. I snuck out in the morning before anyone else woke up." Her face beamed with the sinfulness of it all.

Violet chortled, "Oh Lordy. What'd Shirley say?"

"She said she knew it was bound to happen the way we were flirtin' with each other all night. In fact, she said she'd thought she just help it along by insisting I stay at the Inn overnight too. She reassured me that she was so damned drunk herself, she didn't hear a thing, fell asleep right away. Thank goodness. She also told me it was about damned time I got myself some ... you know ... enjoyment."

"Well, I'll be damned? Ruby Carson got herself some man." Violet slapped her in the leg, "Good for you Honey!" With that, she snuck one more look in Virgil's direction. Luckily, he was looking in hers too.

She waved and smiled at him, and he returned the flirty gesture.

Fran finally joined her friends, "Did I hear right? Ruby's got a man."

"No, had a man." Ruby joked, but by the way, Fran tilted her head, she didn't get it. "Oh, never mind me, what happened with John-Paul?" Ruby winked at Fran, "Come on, spill the beans Franny."

"Well firstly, he gave me this." She held up the cookbook, "He insisted that I have it as a gift." Everyone approved of his kind gesture, with nods and smiles.

"Aaaaand?" prodded Pearl. They slowly made their way down the path towards the station wagon.

She smiled wide, "And he's taking me to dinner tonight, so he can hear all about it." Her eyes gleamed with the thrill of spending an evening with the fetching John-Paul Bordeaux.

Violet squealed, "I knew it! I knew it! I knew it!" She put a halt to her chair by grabbing the wheels, "But wait a darn minute, who asked out who?"

Fran answered bluntly, "He asked, of course. I'm a lady. I don't ask men out on dates." It was apparent that Violet had insulted her virtue.

"Yes! I win!" Violet rubbed her hands together, "Fork it over Pearl." She held up her flat opened hand and grinned greedily. "Ten please?"

"Why in Hades are you the winner? John-Paul was the one who asked her out, she just accepted. So I win!" She shoved her chair hard, "So you owe me ten big fat dollars!"

"Oh no, you don't! I won ..." They continued to argue as they disappeared around the corner of the house and out of sight.

Ruby slapped herself squarely in the forehead, "Oh Lordy, here we go again!"

"Yah, again." Fran reached the corner first. With a twinkle in her eye, she giggled out, "Ten-dollars Violet wins."

Ruby laughed too, "Nope. I got twenty says Pearl wins."

As they vanished around the corner of the farmhouse, the sounds of the laughing and quarreling faded away.

Life on the Lawn

Be sure
to look for
**Kay's newest book
First Page Last Page**
now on sale.

Nitra Zupan faces the one crisis all writers' fear most, losing their entire hand written manuscript weeks before a looming deadline. Worse, she is unable to recapture the essences of her first page, the one she considers to be the most significant page of the entire book. After losing her manuscript to Mother Nature's wrath, she places an ad in the local newspaper offering a reward to have her pages returned to her.

Follow their tense adventure as they encounter the assortment of people who return the pages of her work, only to find them all, except for one. Neither, Nitra nor her house keeper, Wallace McPhee, is aware that the other has feelings that run deeper than their employer, employee relationship. That is, until they encounter the mysterious woman wearing gaudy red lipstick.

The comedic banter between Nitra and Wallace, along with the fast paced adventure, will bring you to the dramatic end of their search for Nitra's first page, the last page.

Be sure to
look for
Kay's previous book
MARKED
now on sale.

George Oscar Dack, a white warlock, is on the verge of shaking up his dull, predictable life. With the help of his sarcastic cat, Darius and a strange old woman, he conducts his experiment using precise elements and implements, to cast a spell upon a Canadian two dollar bill.

Writing his initials across the bill's front as part of the spell, it allows him to observe the bill's travels throughout the day, revealing what effects, either good or corrupt, it has on those who possess it, both young and old characters alike. Some have happy encounters, while others definitely do not.

Come join George and follow the bill's many adventures through his ordinary little town and discover the true connection between him and the old woman who enters into his life.

In the hunt for ...

the perfect martini

KAY D JOHNSON

Be sure
to look for
Kay's previous book

In the hunt for ...
The Perfect Martini!

With a new job and a new life,
middle-aged Izzy Abbott finds herself
lonely and terribly bored.

Each evening, to spice up her life,
she disguises herself in an entirely new identity and visits a different
bar, looking for fun, men, and her version of a dirty dry martini
— her perfect martini.

Even though she is having a blast
on her nightly outings, the recent unsolved murder of a woman in the
city lingers in her mind while she party's. Should she feel secure or
watch out for her safety with a killer on the loose?

Meet the quirky patrons and peculiar bartenders she encounters in
the eclectic drinking establishments she visits.

Come join Izzy in
her zany adventures ... in the hunt for
... the perfect martini.

Be sure
to look for
Kay's Pervious book
Bits Of Blue
Now on sale.

During a marital dispute between tormented Tess and her abusive husband, she finally gathers the courage to fight back for the first time. The result is the unintentional death of Morty Logan. Although it was an accident, Tess was convinced she would be blamed for his gruesome death if she called the authorities.

Determined to stay out of prison for the crime she did not commit, Tess hatched a plan to get rid of the dead body before the summer's heat wave gave her away.

Follow her internal struggles as she disposes of the body, bit by bit, using the one item she had plenty of — little blue zip bags, a sale item her controlling husband demanded she buy by the case.

While doing so, she must hide her true missions from the very nosy neighborhood senior and his friend, the meddlesome cop, both suspiciously watching every move she made.

No one knew what the timid Tess Logan had inside her tote bag as she walked about the city, looking for new places to leave her Bits of Blue

www.ingramcontent.com/pod-product-compliance
Lightning Source LLC
Chambersburg PA
CBHW021111130626
46554CB00002B/638